Saving The Cowboy Way

STEPHANIE B. WHITFIELD

Stephanie B. Whitfield

TO ALL THE COWBOYS AND COWGIRLS OUT THERE.

TABLE OF CONTENTS

Table of Contents

The speed of the wind plastered his hair backward, leaving the sunset behind him. An occasional salty tear escaped his eyes, painting tracks on his cheeks. The horse beneath him flew, her hooves only briefly touching the ground as the mare galloped across the open desert. Dust streaming a brown cloud after them. A quick rhythmic three beat, ba-dum, ba-dum, echoed through his bones and brought joy to his soul.

Parker's family owned a dude ranch in Arizona. They had an agreement with the Native Americans to use their land that boarded the ranch for trail riding and staged cattle drives. They only stayed in Arizona for the cool months. Once May came and the triple digits brought the scorching heat, they took all the horses and cattle to Utah to avoid the summers.

There was something about the desert that spoke to him. When the cacti and wild brush bloomed for the first few weeks in April, there was nothing more beautiful. The vibrant pinks, yellows, and reds, dabbled with baby white flowers randomly scattered over the desert sage greens. The strange silhouette of the saguaro cacti, resembling a stranded hitch hiker in the distance. A romantic aura was created by the sunset with every color of the rainbow.

Dismounting Blossom, he looped her lead rope around the wooden tie rack and unbuckled her cinches. "That's my good girl." Her enormous eye glistened as she licked her lips, showing her rider she loved him back.

"Parker, have you talked to your dad today?" Chase inquired, waiting in the barn. Parker and Chase had been best friends since kindergarten. They were almost brothers. Their families were close. When Chase's parents were killed in a car accident, Parker's dad, Charlie, took him in.

"Do I need to talk to my dad today?" Parker set his saddle on the rack and walked back to his bay mare. He gave her neck a few pats and turned on the hose to rinse the sweat off her coat.

"You might want to hear this one," Chase said, widening both of his eyes. A mischievous grin surfaced.

"Great. It's going to be one of those talks then." Parker untied his wet horse. "I'm tempted to saddle Blossom up again, ride back out into the sunset, and just avoid the entire ordeal."

Chase laughed. Parker led Blossom to the pasture, where he watched her trot off, circle the same spot a few times and then drop to the ground. She rolled around in the dirt, itching herself as she swung back and forth. When she stood, she shook like a giant dog who had just been groomed. Dirt caked onto her wet sides. "I should have left you dirty," he told his horse.

Latching the halter on the post, he walked back to his dad's office. Where he cringed at the thought of what he could have to say to him.

Parker's dad, Charlie, was a hardworking man, and he expected everyone around him to be the same. It wasn't the regular kind of work. This was back-breaking, sweat your butt off, holes in your jeans, blisters on your feet, sunrise to sundown; ranch work.

The cowboy way was dying off, and Parker had found a way to bring it back to life with videos and social media. Allowing people to live it through watching it on their personal devices. He and Chase made a vlog every few days. They documented the work they did on their ranch: the cattle drives, feeding the animals, and the city folk that came to ride on trails.

Their videos were a colossal hit, and they had become well known. Chase was the clown of the two of them. He made everything a joke, his smooth handsome manner swooning every lady in his path. Parker was the real deal. He had roped, rode broncs, and chased cattle since he could walk.

Charlie didn't approve of their videos. His disapproval often led to fights between him and his son. He couldn't believe he would disgrace all the past cowboys in such a fashion. It was an outrage to show their way of life on screens of any kind.

Parker opened the door to his dad's office. He took a deep breath to prepare himself. The tired hinges on the door complained with a loud creak as he walked through. Dirt puffed off his boots as they echoed on the wooden floorboards. His spurs clanged loudly in the silence.

"I could hear you a mile away," Charlie said. He didn't look up from his desk as he continued to log in the day's customers.

Parker licked his chapped lips. He pulled off his cowboy hat and ran his finger through his hair. "You wanted to see me?"

"We've been offered a generous proposal. You know I don't approve of how you and Chase flaunt yourselves all over the internet, but something of worth might finally have come out of it."

One of Parker's eyebrows lifted. He placed his hat back on his head. He shuffled on to his other foot, his spur chimed, and he folded his arms across his chest. It was as if Charlie wanted to torture him. Instead of spitting it out and getting to the point, he stopped talking all together and went back to work. The clock on the wall behind the desk seemed to get louder as he stood there. He would not give him the satisfaction of thinking he was interested. Honestly, he didn't care. His father had given up on him a long time ago. He had moved on, making a new way of life without him to save the ranch. The expenses far outweighing the cost of the land and animals. It wouldn't be much longer before they lost the ranch.

"A representative from Europe called me. They have a princess who is a fan of your ridiculous videography. She wants you to bring the cowboy way to her."

Parker laughed. "You're kidding me?" He sighed and his lips vibrated.

Charlie shook his head. "No, son. This is for real." He pushed a stack of papers across the desk. "This is a contract they've sent. Look it over, sign it, and pack your bags."

"You can't be serious? You think I would travel to some foreign country to prance around and pretend to be a cowboy for a princess?" Parker folded his arms in front of him.

"There will be no pretending, my boy. You are a cowboy. You'll do it because they have offered one hundred thousand dollars and all travel expenses are paid for you and Chase."

Parker's eyes narrowed. "And what part of that hundred thousand belongs to you?" He pointed at his father. "You have never supported the videos we posted. You don't even know what social media is."

"I have officially become your manager." Charlie grinned and folded his arms across his chest.

It took everything inside of Parker to control his anger. Heat rumbled inside of him, his face so hot he was like a volcano, the blistering magma inching closer to explosion. "I'm not going." He spun on his boot heels and left.

Chase was waiting outside the door. He unfolded his arms. Pushing off the building as Parker stormed out the door. Chase rushed after. "Hey wait up."

"Not now, Chase." Parker clenched his jaw and waved his friend off.

"A hundred thousand dogies, my friend. We travel, throw ropes, ride horses, and flirt with princesses." Chase grabbed Parker's arm; he shrugged it off. "What could be so bad about that?"

Parker sighed. "It's not that, it's my dad. He has never supported our videos. He has condoned it. And now he's taking a cut? Hell, for all we know, he's going to take it all."

"Parker, this is a chance of a lifetime. Free travel to Europe. We run the camera, become even more famous, and we leave the old man to run the dude ranch on his own. We do our own thing with the money we make." Chase slapped Parker on the back. "It's us they want. We can change the contract and write the old man out of it."

"Can we do that?"

Chase tipped his cowboy hat. "My friend, you and I can do whatever we want. It's our show, remember?"

Realizing that his friend was right, he gave the thought a chance. Was letting his dad in on the deal such a bad idea? It could help the ranch get back on its feet so they wouldn't have to sell. The thought still made him sick. He loved it here. This ranch was his entire life; it was all he knew. He hated traveling. Leaving the comforts of home wasn't something he was keen on.

CHAPTER 2 THE WET HERO

Parker stretched his arms toward the sky. The horizon held a pale pink and orange hue, with silhouettes of cacti and sagebrush, as the sun rose above the clouds. He sipped on his coffee and walked over to the daily schedule. He eyed the stack of paper that held the Europe contract information.

Tempted to look through it, he pushed his lips together. He resisted, too stubborn to let his old man win. Parker grunted out loud, just in time for Chase to walk in the door, complaining as he did. "Another Park and Chase only ride today?"

"You guessed it." Parker gave Chase a gun finger point.

Chase picked up the stack of papers. It was as thick as a twenty-chapter book. "This is a lot of legal, I wouldn't understand."

"Tell me about," Parker agreed, taking another sip of his coffee.

"Got more of that somewhere?"

"Yup." Parker pointed to the backroom. "I'm not in the mood for giggling fans today."

"Park, it's all part of being famous. We walked into this crap shoot on our own. Signed the book." Chase poured himself a cup. "Dang, man, this coffee is excellent."

"It's all about the temperature and measuring it out, precisely."

"So, you mean dumping it in and guessing is bad?"

Parker shook his head. Typical Chase, he was all about convenience. He took each day with a wish and a prayer. He never read the instructions, or did things in the right order. It was the Chase-way. He flirted with every female regardless of her relationship status. He didn't care. If she was in his path, she was in the books.

The guys finished their coffee and headed out to saddle the horses. They were a full operation ranch. There were beef cattle, cattle they used for roping, and pretend cattle drives for the paid customers. This also meant they had over thirty horses, which allowed options for the visitors to get the full cowboy experience.

"Did you send a text to Jason?" Parker inquired.

Jason was the background guy. He was the silent partner who did all the camera and video editing. Jason wasn't great on a horse, but he managed when they needed him to.

"Of course I did," Chase said. "I'm not always a poor planner." Chase placed a saddle on one of the four horses. "He's going to have to come with us to Europe, you know?"

"I haven't decided on that yet," Parker grumbled, and finished buckling up the last horse. He walked out to the pasture where he had let Blossom out the evening before. She nickered. "Hey, my pretty girl." She bobbed her head up and down as she slowly moseyed over to the gate.

Parker patted her neck and gave his mare a treat he had stashed in his pocket. She gladly accepted. He placed a halter over her head and led her to the tie station. He looped her rope around the bar close to Chase's big gelding. "How am I going to be a good cowboy without my best girl here?"

Two blue eyes peeked out from over the tall, 16.2 hand gray gelding named Grey. "They have horses in Europe." Chase chuckled. "Blossom will be here when we get back."

Huffing, Parker pressed his lips together. "Yeah, pretty boy horses. They don't have western saddles over there, you know? And they wear yoga pants, not jeans."

"Ok? And you're complaining about princesses in yoga pants?" Chase walked around his horse. "Listen, you're overthinking this whole thing. Just let me handle this, okay?" He put a hand on Parker's shoulder, squeezing. "This is going to be a great experience. Worst case, the video coverage we get will knock people's socks off. And remember, women in yoga pants isn't a bad thing."

Adjusting his hat, Parker chuckled. Defeated, he could not deny, there was nothing wrong with women in tight stretchy pants. Parker mumbled to himself. "I'll look over the papers." He nodded his head. "And the men wear the yoga pants, too."

Chase jumped in the air, cha-chinging one of his arms in a victory dance. "It's going to be great. I promise. Just think, this could be our ticket to freedom."

Two cars pulled up in the parking lot and then a third behind them. "There are our riders," Parker said. "And there's Jason, right on time."

Jason's arms were full of camera equipment. He stumbled, trying to close the trunk of his car. Jason was plump around his mid-section. He sat behind a computer most of the time, and the only time he got out was when he helped Chase and Parker make videos. Chase ran over to help him.

Four college-aged women scrambled out of the other two cars, chatting away with one another. One of them screamed, holding her hands over her mouth as she ran over to Chase. She did a little happy dance as she looked at her friends. She waved at them to get their phones out for a photo.

"Oh my, oh my," she squealed, still bouncing. "It's Chase!" She screamed, her excitement at meeting someone famous was too much to handle.

Chase tipped his hat. "Ma'am."

She swooned into her friends, who had now joined her. "Can we please get a picture?" she begged.

"Why, of course you can, dear."

Parker rolled his eyes and shook his head. "What a smoozer. Look at him Blossom." The bay mare looked at her owner. "Don't give me that glare. Why would I ever be jealous of that?"

"Parker, get over here!" Chase called from the squabble of woman, who were practically petting his chest and arms. Their cameras snapping over and over off selfie sticks.

Parker declined, grumbling to himself. "Get those ladies inside to sign waivers. There is time to take pictures later."

One of them waved. "Hi Parker."

Tipping his hat, he acknowledged her. He really disliked this part of his dad's business. It wasn't as annoying before he and Chase had become famous on the internet. He had done that to himself. Back then, he was just a good-looking cowboy taking people on rides. Now it was drooling, touching, "take my picture," "sign my boots" or whatever else they could show off to their social media posts.

Strapping the last saddle bag and placing Jason's equipment onto Biscuit, Parker finished bridling the other horses. He finished just in time for them to walk outside after signing waivers. When the door creaked and the voices of excitement over Chase covered the silence he loved so much, he sighed.

As they walked over, Parker shook his head at Chase. He was grinning ear to ear with an armful of women. He gave Parker the stink eye, warning him to not say anything to ruin his fun. Parker knew this was his cue to suck it up and put on his famous face. "Howdy ladies." He tipped his hat.

Two of them ran from Chase and almost plowed Parker over. Their excitement shook him. He really needed to find a no-touchy clause and add it to the waivers they signed. They hung on his arms and petted him as the other two girls snapped pictures. He smiled and played along with the game while secretly brooding inside.

Chase joined in and they asked Jason to take a few snapshots of all of them, together with both cowboys.

"Did you ladies want pictures on the horses, too?" Jason asked.

They all agreed, and Jason took a few more before they started out for the trail. The horses any of the paid customers rode were well seasoned and not in a hurry to get anywhere fast. They followed one another, head to tail, in a single file line. Never allowed to go faster than a walk. This was all for safety.

Chase took the lead, and Parker followed along the side, making sure everyone stayed safe. Jason took the rear, ready to fire up the camera when the time was right.

"So, Parker," one of the blonde customers inquired. "Are you dating? I mean, you know we watch your videos, but," she winked, "we don't get to know what is going on in your personal life?"

That was bold, he thought to himself. His chocolate brown eyes against his olive skin met hers and he thought she might fall off her horse. Parker and Chase weren't just famous because they had a cowboy channel. Both men were athletic, kept their bodies healthy, muscles well defined, with faces of super models. Any girl in her right mind would call them heart-throbs.

Chase was blond, his hair a longer cut, thickly curled under the edge of his cowboy hat. His blue eyes were light, almost piercing. Whereas, Parker was his opposite, the tall, dark, and handsome type. His dark brown, coffee bean hair was kept short. His eyes were a chocolate color, warm and inviting.

Smiling, Parker nodded his head once. She took in a large breath and held her hand to her heart. "Don't drop your reins, ma'am." She quickly retracted them, fumbling to gather them up. "To answer your question, the only lady I need in my life right now is Blossom." He reached down and patted the mare's neck.

"That is the cutest thing I have ever heard." She batted her eyes. "Heather, my friend up there," she pointed to the front horse, "really likes the bold guys, like Chase, but you, you are the hopeless romantic. The silent, handsome one in the background. The support system who keeps it all together. Now that is what I'm into."

He wanted to roll his eyes, but this lady was a paying customer. So, instead, he smiled and tipped his hat, ignoring the strong come on. He nudged Blossom to speed up and stopped on the side of the trail. "Ladies, up here soon we will cross the river. When doing so, don't let your horses, drink, or paw. They are well fed and watered. This is not an invitation for them to play splash. This means they are warning you they are going to take you for a dip in the water."

Two of the ladies gasped, giving one another looks of horror. Their eyes widened, and the color of their faces going pale for a moment. "Just nudge them forward with your leg and keep them walking." He nodded to Chase, who was waving his hat in the air. "Just follow the big blond idiot up there. Do as he does, or maybe don't." He chuckled.

Parker nodded to Jason to start the videotaping. This was when it always got good. Chase led the small herd of horses, easing his big gray into the water one step at a time. "Lean back and put your feet in front of you as the horse steps down the slope."

The first three horses followed Grey, but the fourth horse with the lady who had tried to smooth talk to

Parker stopped. He brought up his right hoof and pawed. Splashing water on anything within three feet of him. The blonde on his back screamed. She dropped her reins as she waved her hands in the air. Panicking, she grabbed the saddle horn; her knuckles bulging white.

"Miss, you need to hold his reins and keep him moving," Parker pleaded with her. "Move your horse forward!" He nudged Blossom closer to help pull the splashing gelding, but he was too late. The red horse dropped, dunking his rider into the river with him. Her yell for help was half muffled as she submerged with the horse.

The blonde surfaced from the river, soaked, and screaming. "I hate horses! Why would he do that?"

It took everything Parker had to not laugh. That was one of the funniest things he had seen in a long time. He dismounted Blossom, who stood waiting for him to come back. He walked over to her and helped lift her, placing his hands gently under her armpits, and guided her out of the strong current in the river.

"Are you injured anywhere?" Parked asked her.

"Only mentally traumatized," she said, flailing her arms around his neck. The water from her river-soaked clothing transferred to his own. "Oh, Parker. You're my hero."

Parker's eyes widened. Unsure if he should push her away, afraid to offend her and lose a customer, he stayed. He fought the urge to drop her back into the water. She slammed a peck on his check, her soft lips, froze him like an ice cube, his feet bracing them both on the rocky riverbed, against the soft watery current.

She continued to kiss him, his eyes beaming like a scared deer.

Chills formed on his neck and arms. It had been a long time since a woman had kissed him. And this was not something he had invited or wanted from this one. This was sexual harassment at its finest. She had taken him in a vulnerable moment. Used him. Had she done it on purpose to get closer to him?

With a quick glance at Jason, he had remembered this was all on camera. Even if he paid Chase to delete it, he wouldn't. Chase was going to blast this to the world, use it to every advantage. He had to make light of it and play along. He swung an arm under her legs and swooped her off her feet.

She squealed; her eyes sparkled like firecrackers as she stared at the handsome cowboy in front of her. He walked her over to Blossom, placed her on the horse's back, and swung up behind of her. He clucked his bay mare forward, led her toward the edge of the water, where the red gelding now stood wet and enjoying his pick of food.

Like lightning, Parker leaned over, grabbed the reins, and pulled the sorrel behind them out of the water. The crowd on the sidelines cheered and clapped as they neared the edge. Parker dismounted, held up both arms to the blonde and helped her down off his horse. "Did you need any help with mounting your horse?"

"I'm not getting back on that beast. I prefer to ride with you." She smiled and batted her eyes. He swore she moved her hips closer to his own.

Parker glanced over at Chase for help. He gave none. Instead, Chase laughed, enjoying the show even though he knew his friend was having a hard time. "I am sorry… Um, what did you say your name was?"

"Krissy."

"Miss Krissy, it would be a lot to ask Blossom to carry two riders. You'll have to ride back on Red here or walk. He really is a good boy."

"Are you saying I'm fat?"

"Shoot! No. I was…"

"You are! You cussed too!"

"No, Ma'am. I was thinking of the horse."

"You're choosing the beast over me?" She held her forearm to her head. "I can't believe your horse is more important. I felt a spark between us. Did you not feel it too?"

"Uh… Ma'am… I." Parker's shoulders sagged slightly. There was no winning with this gal. He wanted to jump back on Blossom and run to high heaven to escape this awful drama he was stuck in. The worst part was, he knew Jason was still filming.

"Krissy, give poor Parker a break." Chase reined Grey over to the side of Red. "He has to ride Blossom here all day long. He's only trying to keep her from getting sore legs. It has nothing to do with weight, more to do with practicality. How would you feel walking up and down these trails all day carrying that big cowboy? Then, to add another body, it's just asking a lot of the mare."

The woman eyed the blond, blue-eyed cowboy on the gray horse. "Well, I guess if you put it that way?"

"Parker meant no offense by it," Chase said, stealing a wink at his friend.

Closing his eyes Parker, silently thanked his friend. Grateful he held so much charisma to pull him out of this disaster. He couldn't wait for the day to end.

Huffing, she walked over to the red gelding. "I don't know how to get on this," she waved her hand over the horse, "by myself."

Parker walked over, leading Blossom behind him. He bent over and made a cup shape with his hands. "Step here and then into that stirrup. Grab onto the horn and pull yourself up."

"You want me to step into your hands?"

"Yes, Ma'am."

Rolling her eyes, Krissy did as he asked. Mounted her horse and didn't look back. They rode the rest of the trail. After the water incident, Krissy had no desire to talk to Parker again. He was relieved. Though he knew he would have to pretend the stolen kisses didn't bother him.

After the four women had left. The three men sat around the office couches, taking a break from the long day. "I have some great footage of that Krissy lady," Jason added.

Parker took off his hat, sat it on his knee and shook his head. He rubbed at his temples, feeling the dirt that clung to his skin.

"You should see the look on Parker's face when she kissed him. I thought he was going to poop himself." Jason shifted his leg to cross over his knee. "I think our next video title should be how to kiss a wet cowboy."

"How to make a cowboy wet," Chase added, laughing hysterically after. "What do to with a drenched cowboy?" Chase sat up, tracing imaginary lettering in the air. "Or how to make a cowboy poop himself?"

They laughed. Parker was not amused.

"All right, all right. Enough. I don't normally have to deal with the customers. Usually, they all flock to Chase. I'm the one that ropes and rides the bucking bulls. Not that guy who saves the lady in distress. I froze. I didn't know what to do or how to act."

"It's okay, Parker, take one for the team this time. This is going to be classic. The lady fans are going to love it." Chase slapped his friend on the back, Parker's hat popped off his knee and thudded to the ground. "You need more practice with the opposite sex, my brother."

Parker picked up his hat. He turned it around to check for damages before he put it back on his head in a safe place. Maybe his friend was right. Deep inside him, he knew he needed to move on. The attention he wanted from a lady wasn't the kind he experienced today. He wanted it to be genuine. He wanted it to mean something.

Chapter 3 Another Cattle Drive

The next morning, Parker took his truck into town. He left Chase to run the ranch. He really didn't want to deal with a repeat of yesterday. The town's only diner was about twenty minutes away. He visited often to get away from the hustle of work.

The door chimed when he walked in. The older lady behind the counter had curled hair that rolled up under her vintage nippy, a short hat that covered most of her hair. Pointed glasses protruded past the wrinkles on the sides of her face. She had worked there since he was a kid. Her mama owned it before her and now she had taken over. "Morn'n Parker."

"Morning Flo. Could I get the usual?"

"You bet, sweetie."

Choosing to sit at the booth he always sat at, in the back corner, he stared out the window. Maybe Chase was right. The change that this Europe deal could bring might be good. An opportunity he might be sorry he passed up. It would give him a break from the annoying fans who came to the ranch.

"What'cha got on your mind, cowboy?" Flo asked as she set down a porcelain mug and poured in the steamy black coffee.

His brown eyes met hers and even though she could be his grandmother, the handsome young man in front of her was attractive. Her cheeks flushed, and a wide smile spread across her lips.

"I have been pondering a business opportunity. It might be out of my comfort zone, but I'm seriously considering."

"Ya-know, let me tell you something about what Ol' Flo here has learned. Life brings us chances. We don't always get to choose the good ones. Sometimes they hit you in the face like a brick, other times we wish we had picked up the brick." She set a hand on Parker's shoulder. "I think you should pick up the brick this time son, don't let it hit you in the face later."

Bringing the mug up to his lips, he took a gentle sip. "I think you're right, Flo. Thank you."

"Anytime kid." She winked. "Let me go get your pancakes and bacon. They should be ready." She patted his shoulder and walked off.

After finishing his breakfast, Parker paid Flo and took a walk. The small town he had grown up to know was changing. People came from all around to visit. Old buildings were being restored and renovated into social media attractions for visitors. Parker agreed all this was good for the economy, but at some point, this is how the cowboy way of life got to where it was today, a thing of the past; pushed out and forgotten.

A pain in his heart caused him to stop. He took an enormous sigh and watched a roadrunner dash across the street. "Enjoy the freedom while you can, my friend."

"Is that?" a young girl asked, pointing at Parker. He looked behind him, finding only himself in the direction they were pointing. Alone. No Chase to save him. "It is!" She squealed, grabbing her friend's arm, dragging her in toward him.

Great, he thought. He had left the ranch to get away from this. There was no escape. He tipped his hat at the two teens, who still stood staring and whispering.

"Can we get a selfie with you?" one of them asked.

"Uh... sure."

The two girls slammed in to him, one on each side. It took effort not to grunt from their abrupt joining. The cowboy smiled, no teeth, just giving a tough side lip upward. They snapped several shots as they posed with him like he was a statue. He could feel his insides trembling. Cowboys were strong. They never allowed weakness to show outwardly.

"Thank you. Where is Chase?" Of course, they'd ask about Chase.

"He's uh, back at the ranch." Parker awkwardly pointed a thumb over his shoulder in the wrong direction. Silently cursing himself for being dumb.

"I thought you two were like, never apart."

"Well, um, I needed some thinkin' time."

"Oh my gosh, you're like so hot!" the girl said, almost falling over on her friend.

Parker felt the blood rush to his face. He rubbed the back of his neck and shuffled his right boot on the ground. "Uh thanks?"

"Could we like come to the ranch with you and meet Chase?"

"Well, you could call and make an appointment." Parker rubbed his chin with his thumb and pointer finger. "We get pretty busy, so setting up a time is best."

They whispered something to one another. "Thanks Parker." They interlocked arms and scurried off. Europe was looking better and better by the minute. Maybe there he wouldn't have to deal with all the squealing girls.

When Parker arrived back at the ranch. Chase was unsaddling the horses that had just been out on the trail. "Hey my brother. How was your breakfast?"

"It was much needed." Parker pulled off the saddle Chase had unbuckled. "Have you had time to look over that contract?"

"I did a little. It's a lot of protect the princess crap."

"I think we should go." Parker set the saddle on its place on the rack.

Chase put an arm around his friend, bringing him into a side hug. "I knew you would come to your senses. This is going to be a blast."

"I'm ready for a change. I keep telling myself the world I love so much isn't going to affect how I feel. So instead of letting it slowly kick us out, let's grab it by the balls, embrace it and come out fighting with two fists on the other side."

"That's my man," Chase said, nodding his head. "That is the cowboy way."

Parker finished helping Chase unsaddle, put away the horses, and then went into the office. He grabbed the stack of papers that made up the contract and stared at it. Almost willing it to change somehow. He was glad the desk was empty, so he wouldn't have to hear his father. He placed the stack under his arm and turned to leave. Only to stop dead in his track as the squeaky door let his father in.

"Oh, good Parker, I have been meaning to talk with you." Charlie's eyes dropped to the pile under Parker's arm. "I see you have finally talked yourself into some sense."

"Yes, about that..."

Charlie held up a hand to interrupt his son. "I have pondered our recent chat. And I realize that I have been hard on you, and I haven't told you enough how proud I am of the man you have become."

"Dad, you don't have to..."

"No. I do. Parker, I didn't see the value in what you and Chase did until after I got to watching some of your videos. The two of you have shown the world what being a cowboy is like. Sadly, it's going to be the only thing that might give us some hope."

"I don't always agree with how Chase does things, but the people love it," Parker added.

"I know. I have been watching." Charlie outstretched a hand and placed it on his son, and looked him in the eyes. "I'm not going to take your money. The two of you have worked hard to earn every penny. But I think you should take this chance to travel, learn, and live. If you help the ranch with it, that is your choice."

"Thanks Dad." Parker was surprised. How had a man with such a hard heart soften, so quickly? Money? Or was it old age? He didn't know, but he liked it.

"I had my lawyer look over the contract. He added a few things to protect you boys and get Jason paid for, too. Sign it and we will have them look it over. If all goes well, the three of you boys will be headed to Europe in a week."

Parker pulled off his hat and scratched at his dark brown hair. "Wow, that seems awful soon."

"Son, they are ready and waiting."

"Dad?"

Charlie looked up at his son from his desk.

"Will you make sure Blossom is taken care of? I don't want anyone to ride her until I get back."

"I promise." Charlie laced his fingers together over his desk and smiled.

Tipping his hat, Parker walked out. The wooden door hinges complaining behind him.

***

The next morning came too quickly. A prominent company paid to have a group of fifty customers taken on a guided cattle drive. The ranch had to borrow horses from a friend of Charlie's because they didn't have that many trail horses. Jason packed his video equipment into the chuck wagon with the cook. His view from the wagon would be far superior to that of the back of a horse.

This event was an entire day. Parker woke up a few hours early that morning and drove ten cattle out to the range and staged them. The customers would ride out in a few hours to find them, herd them into a corral, and then head back to the stable to finish with a dinner.

As the sun rose behind him, Parker slowly loped Blossom back to the ranch house. He hoped she wouldn't miss him too much while he was gone. He knew he was going to miss her. The Europe trip was going to seem like forever. They would be gone for a month.

When he arrived back, he joined in with Chase and two other hired hands in saddling the horses. The customers started piling in just before lunch. The cook had smoked pulled pork and the aroma of burned mesquite wood lingered in the air. Once the group had signed the liability waivers, they could sit and have lunch.

Chase, Jason, and Parker sat at a far table with the other two hands, Scott, and Kyle. They watched the city folk eating, talking, and adjusting their newly bought boots and jeans. Some of them had even gone as far to buy chaps. They took extra measures to get the complete experience.

"I bet that one there gets off halfway," Kyle said, covering his mouth so only the hands could hear his voice.

"Money down. The blonde in the pink boots falls off," Scott added.

"If her shirt were any tighter, it might rip open when she bounces on top of her horse," Kyle said. All of them laughed.

"Come on, boys, let's get these folks on some horses," Parker interrupted, standing up from the table.

With such a large group of people, more than half of them had never sat on a horse. A small part of them had only ridden in little circles at a fair as a kid. "Hello everyone, I hope you're all ready for a fun cowboy experience. For those of you have not ridden before, you'll want to keep your body in the center of the saddle, sort of like riding a bike," Parker said.

Each of the wranglers helped place the riders on a horse. Helping them to mount and show the basics. "These are the reins. You hold them with both hands.

Left to go left, right to go right, and pull straight back to stop or slow down." Parker repeated this same sentence several times.

Chase leaned into Parker's left ear as they walked between customers. "This is going to be a really long day."

"Seriously, make sure Jason is ready." Parker walked away toward Blossom and stopped. "Actually, maybe he just shouldn't stop filming."

Jason gave him the thumbs up. He reached back behind him inside the chuck wagon and grabbed out the camera bag. He was sitting shotgun next to the cook so he would have a superb view.

Chase took the lead with Grey and the rest of the horses followed head to tail while Parker, Kyle, and Scott rode along the sides, making sure no one was falling off or breaking rules.

"We have three basic rules to follow while riding. First, don't fall off. Second, stay in your line and walk only, until instructed. Going any other speed than walking excites the horses, which could cause horses going too fast for riders who aren't as comfortable riding. This is for everyone's safety. Third, let's all have some fun," Kyle said as he rode up and down the line.

"Can I get a Yee-hah?" Scott asked.

A few of them followed, yelling out their best Yee-hah. Others chuckled, feeling it was silly. Parker shook his head, hiding his smile under the brim of his hat as he tipped his head downward. He nudged Blossom to a trot to catch up with Chase.

"Hey man. How's it looking back there?" Chase asked.

"So far, so good. No casualties yet. I'm sure glad we aren't crossing the river." Parker pulled out his rope and began twirling it around to give the guests a show. More like he was showing off, but this was something he enjoyed doing.

"How much further?" Scott asked as Parker passed him.

"Only about a ten-minute ride. I left them right around the watering hole."

As Parker headed back, he noticed one rider leaning to the side. He quickly looped his rope back on his saddle. It was a larger man who he had helped mount up earlier. He was terrified and his hands had been shaking. He held a death grip on the saddle horn; the reins tucked under his white knuckles.

"Sir, can I help you get your saddle straight? You're leaning a little to the left there." Parker cocked his head to the side. The man met his eyes. They were wide, his face emotions wiped clean. "It's all right. We just want to make sure you stay on straight. If you just lean your weight a little on that right stirrup, it should help straighten it up."

The man leaned, but quickly retracted back to his white knuckled hold on the horn. He shook his head and stayed like an ice block frozen in place as the horses' walk rocked him back and forth.

Parker knew they needed to get the saddle back in line or eventually it was going to slip and the rider would fall. "What is your name, sir?"

"M-m, Michael."

"Give me two minutes to get the line stopped and we'll get you fixed up." Parker packed up his rope and spun Blossom, kicking her forward, back toward the front. "Chase? We have a leaner back there. Can we hold up for a moment?"

"Sure thing, boss," Chase said, tilting his hat.

Heading back, one rider asked, "Hey why are we stopping?"

"Just a quick adjustment. Hang tight a sec."

When he reached the poor man. Michael was near falling. Parker dismounted Blossom at a trot, knowing he had no time to get off her the normal way. A few of the guests "oohed." He raced over as fast as he could, spooking none of the horses, but he was too late.

The man panicked, his weight transferred to the leaning saddle and to adjust to Michael's weight, the horse under him hastened to the opposite direction. This sent the rider toppling to the ground. Parker was fast, but not fast enough.

Wincing Parker, knew the man was going to be hurting. "Are you alright?" He was at his side, dusting off his back and helping him to rise.

"I think I'm okay. Can I make a request to ride in the cook wagon instead?" Michael brushed more dirt off his jeans. "Horses really aren't my jam."

"Sure thing. I'll have Jason switch you spots." Parker helped Michael check for any injuries he might have incurred with the fall. Except for some scrapes and bruises, he would be fine.

Parker jogged over to Blossom, who had found some grasses to eat. Grabbing the horn, he swung his right leg up and over with little to no effort. Spun his bay mare around and quickened her pace to the chuck wagon.

"Dude, Parker, I got that whole thing on video." Jason lifted his free arm in his excitement and slapped it back down on his thigh. "Parker, the cowboy hero to the rescue."

Shaking his head, a small smile escaped Parker's lips. He really didn't want any credit for doing the right thing. "Jason, could you swap spots with our fallen rider? He's a little beat up."

"Yeah, sure thing. Let me grab my things and pack them into the saddlebags."

John, the cook, turned the wagon around and met up with the fallen Michael. They laced the camera equipment on to the trail horse, and they helped Michael climb up next to John. "Thanks for letting me come up here instead. My place really is with the food."

"No problem, man," John said, snapping his reins over the top of the two black draft horses. "Come on, boys." He winked. "Just glad you weren't seriously hurt."

"All right, let's get this show on the road and find us some cattle to round up," Parker said, bringing his rope back out and waving it in the air. He twirled it above him, then let the rope slide through the hondo; the small rawhide hole at the end. The loop grew large enough to circle around Blossom. He kept it swirling around her as she walked up the sides of the trail line.

"That is incredible. I'm Katie."

"Why thank you, Miss Katie," Parker said, tipping his hat. He watched her face redden when he gave her a wink. Twirling it around upward, it got smaller. He shifted the rope to above him, showing off a little more, bringing it over to both sides of his mare. He brought the rope back up and, like magic, he had it back into a small gathered bundle at the side of his saddle.

Katie was now five shades of red. The gorgeous cowboy next to her was eye candy at its finest. She could only dream of dating someone like him. "Do you mind?" She held up her phone.

"No, go right ahead." Parker cocked his head to the side and held out his hand in a hang loose sign as she snapped a few pictures.

"Thank you so much," Katie told him.

"I see some cattle up here folks," Chase called from the front of the line. "Keep your horses walking. If we go too fast, it'll spook the cows and cause a stampede." He reined Grey to face the riders. "You're now allowed to come out of the line. If we can spread out in a semi-circle behind and to the side of them, I'll try to get to the lead and help bring them to a holding pen. We have about half a mile to drive them from here."

The guest riders spread out and angled their horses to the cattle. One by one, the cattle stopped grazing and slowly moseyed toward the gray horse and his blond cowboy.

"Did you have time to see Parker and Chase up close?" Katie asked her co-worker.

"Not yet. One of the other guys helped me mount up. Which one is hotter?"

Parker smiled, listening in on the conversation that went on not too far ahead of him.

Katie blew out a huff. "Well, take your pick, tall, dark and broody or blond, blue-eyed surfer in a cowboy hat."

Parker kicked Blossom forward. "Ladies," he said, tipping his hat as he rode by. Both ladies gasped as he rode by.

The rest of the cattle drive was uneventful. They pushed the cattle back into the holding pen, which was the corral they always stayed in. A little secret the paid guests didn't know. The story was now the shipping truck could come pick the cows up and take them to auction. The even funnier part was that these cattle were not even beef cattle. They were a smaller breed normally used for recreational sports like roping or, in this case, to give a paid customer the satisfaction of going on a real cattle drive.

The wranglers helped all the guests dismount and showed them to the cleaning stations. John then pulled out his pots and pans from the chuck wagon and cooked a dinner of steak, cowboy beans, a roll, and a soda or beer of choice. Of course, it was mostly a show because with that large of a party, it would take forever for one man to cook all of that food in a few pots and pans. So, the kitchen at the main camp helped.

Parker grabbed his plate and walked out to the pasture where he kept Blossom. He sat down with his back against a tree and forked at his steak. His bay mare wandered over slowly. "Hey pretty girl." He pulled out a carrot he had grabbed from the kitchen. He snapped it in half with a loud crack; Blossom perked up her ears and sped up her walk, eagerly anticipating her treat.

Her sand paper muzzle tickled his hand as she took the carrot, instantly nudging him for the other half. "You should chew your food before you take another bite, you know? It's not ladylike." She bobbed her head up and down. Parker chuckled and gave her what she wanted with a loving pat on her neck. When she knew he was all out of horse snacks, she walked off to munch on grasses nearby.

"Over here all alone again?" Chase asked. He sat down next to his friend. "You know we could get a lot more subscribers if you were less," Chase waved his hand through the air, "introverted, hanging out with only Blossom. And maybe talked to people more?"

Parker pulled at his roll. He watched Chase but said nothing.

"Are you sure about this trip? I don't want to take you away from this, if this makes you happy," Chase asked.

Swallowing his bite of roll, Parker took a deep breath. "I have thought about it. The change will be good. I'll miss it sure. Maybe, just maybe, this will open some new doors. Bring in more subscribers and help the ranch get in a better place financially."

Chase slapped his friend on the back, almost causing him to choke on the bite he had just taken. "Oh, my brother, you have no idea. We are going to rock it."

CHAPTER 4 BOOT REMOVAL

Parker woke the morning they would leave with his stomach in knots. He had never flown on an airplane before. He was a land creature. Why on earth would he want to go hundreds of feet in the sky in a metal death trap? He also hated leaving Blossom. Yes, his dad promised to take care of her, but his dad was also one to forget he had made them.

Pressing his lips together, he stared at his long-time friend and most trusted tool; his saddle. The large piece of tooled leather was a part of him. He had sat in it, trusted it with his life for over fifteen years. It was like an extension of him. He could haul it to Europe with him, never letting it leave his side. There was no way he could trust it wouldn't arrive unharmed if he checked it through baggage. Would it even fit through the x-ray machines?

He had heard the horror stories of bags getting lost or stolen. He also knew the airline workers could not care less if luggage held precious cargo inside. They would toss, throw, and chuck every piece of luggage that was to enter the bottom of the plane. And the tree of a saddle could easily be broken. Once that happened, it was worthless.

Chase popped his head into the bedroom door. He found Parker standing there, still staring at his saddle. "I promise you, my man, they will have saddles on the other side of the ocean."

"I just feel so wrong leaving it here. It's a part of me. I could just take it as my carry on?"

"Let's go. Leave it behind. Lock the door. It'll be here waiting when you get back."

Nine hours on a plane… Worst way to travel ever. Parker was ready to jump out the window by the time they landed. His knees were stiff and his head felt like someone had hit him with a bag of feed. The three guys grabbed their carry-on bags and headed toward the baggage claim. Chase and Parker had everything they needed in the bag over their shoulders. Jason's equipment was the only item they had carefully packed and checked to travel under the plane.

Once they retrieved his bags, they walked toward the exit doors to find a man dressed in a suit holding a sign: Chase Winters, Parker Hawkins, and Jason Ford. The three of them stuck out like a sore thumb. Their blue jeans, dirty boots and cowboy hats weren't something you would expect to see, except maybe off a movie screen.

The suited man waved them over. "Gentlemen. We've been expecting you. How was your flight?"

Parker eyed Chase, doing his best not to laugh at his strange accent. "It was long."

The man chuckled. "Well, yes, you traveled a long way. I'm Carson. I work for Her Royal Highness. She has instructed me to bring you to your quarters." He rolled his neck, a crack followed.

They followed Carson outside of the airport to a black limo. He opened the door, bent over slightly, and gestured for them to enter. "I feel a little weird letting a man open my door," Parker whispered to Chase.

Chase's chest bounced up and down as he agreed with his friend. Carson got into the driver's seat after he closed the door behind them. He leaned over before he started the car and faced the three cowboys. "All drinks are complementary. Please help yourselves, gentlemen."

A window then rolled up. Closing them off from the driver. "Well, that there is fancy," Chase said, as he opened the small drink bar. "What the heck is all of this? I have never seen the likes of these."

"That's because we are on the other side of the ocean." Parker grabbed what looked some version of a fancy ginger-ale. He popped it open and took a sip. "Now that is what I'm talking about."

"Hand me one of those," Jason said.

The three of them sat back, enjoyed their drinks and eventually all three of them passed out, snoring. A long plane trip wasn't a place to get a good sleep.

***

A clearing of the throat awoke them. "I hope you enjoyed the car ride?" Carson stood at the side of the car with an open door. "If you could please exit, I will show you to your cottage."

With heavy feet, they dragged themselves out of the stretched car. The chilled air sliced through Parker's jeans and button-down shirt like a sword straight to the heart. A chill attempted to make its way down his spine, but he was too tough to show a weakness for cold weather. His skin betrayed him with tiny bumps that appeared on his exposed skin. They weren't in the hot Arizonian desert any more.

"Holy crap, it's cold here," Chase admitted. He rubbed his arms up and down to bring his skin some warmth. Jason was speechless. Standing like a stump, holding his bags, and squeezing his arms as close to his body as humanly possible.

"I would imagine the weather is a change from where you are from." Carson opened the lock to the cozy cottage door with a large vintage key. "This will be your place of rest during your stay. Her highness's birthday is in a few days. She will expect to see you then. In the meantime, please feel free to get adjusted, learn about your surroundings and so on. There is a cook, and maid that will attend to you here. And there will be a young lad to show you around in the morning. It has been a pleasure. Please enjoy your stay." Carson bowed, turned on his heels, and headed back to the car.

The three of them stood in the doorway, groggy from the long trip. "Did you guys just feel like we got some kind of royal treatment?" Chase asked, with one eyebrow raised.

"That was weird." Parker pushed his way through his friends and into the door. "A cook and a maid? What have we been missing, boys?" Walking straight into the main room, he dropped his bag on the floor and plopped on the couch.

The cottage was quaint but homey. A small gathering area surrounded a stone fireplace in the entrance. A kitchen sat off to the right. Parker opened the refrigerator to find it fully stocked. "Wow. You boys hungry?"

Parker pulled out a cheese block and bit into it. "Holy smoke-balls, this is the best cheese ever." He left the kitchen into a hallway that led past a bathroom and then into two bedrooms. Each one was small, with one twin sized bed and a dresser. The third room was on the other side of the kitchen.

Chase followed Parker. He grabbed the cheese from his hand and bit into the soft flesh. "Wow," he said, his mouth full still, "you weren't kidding." Chase set his bag down. "This is my room."

"I'll take the one on the other side," Jason called out from the main room.

"I guess that leaves me the one closest to the bathroom," Parker said, walking out of Chase's claimed room. He entered the small room. Setting his bag on the bed, he sat down, the soft mattress buckled with his weight. He looked around. The walls were wallpapered in stripes. Vintage, he thought. Paintings of fox hunts, riders in funny saddles and a stuffed pheasant attached to the walls.

Still tired from the plane ride over, he placed his hat carefully on the dresser, kicked off his boots, sat his bag on the ground and folded his arms behind his head. Before he knew it, he was fast asleep.

The smell of breakfast woke him up. Parker pulled on clean clothes and freshened in the bathroom. After he walked into the kitchen to find a plump, curly haired woman with a flower apron on cooking in the kitchen.

"Oh! Good morn'n lad."

He pressed his lips together to conceal a laugh. "Good morning."

"I have done my best to get ye American breakfast as close as I could to what ye used to." She held a spoon up in the air, waiting for him to reply. "I'm Ethel, your cook."

"Nice to meet you, Ethel. I'm Parker."

"Oh deary, you're the one the princess fancies. I can see why." Ethel quickly held her hand to her mouth. "I shouldn't have said that."

This time, Parker laughed. "It's okay. I have gotten used to it. Breakfast smells great, by the way."

"Are you hungry? I have a plate made up for you here?" Ethel brought a plate of caramel colored toast, a boiled egg in a silly metal holder, scrambled eggs and a side of butter and jam. "I had a block of cheese to cut up, but they must have forgotten to stock it."

Biting his lip, he admitted to taking the cheese. "I'm sorry. After all that traveling, I was hungry. I think Chase finished it."

"No worries, deary. I'll have them restock a few more," Ethel said, winking at the cute cowboy.

Chase walked into the kitchen, still half asleep. He had only pulled on jeans, his chiseled abs flexed as he rubbed his eyes. The blond hair on his head spiked out like a cactus in all directions. He bumped into the table before he found a chair.

"Did you sleep okay, Prince Charming?" Parker asked, laughing a little at his friend.

"I could use a few more hours." Chase sat down. "The smell of food was too good," he rubbed the skin on his stomach, "the growling was loud, so I had to get up."

Ethel brought him a plate. "Good Morn'n, I'm Ethel, the cook. Please let me know if there's anything you'd like. I can add to the menu while you boys are here."

"More of that cheese I ate last night? Make every dish with it," Chase teased. He shoveled a spoonful of eggs into his mouth.

Laughing, her belly bounced. Ethel rubbed her hands on her apron. "I'll make sure we add more cheese to the list."

"We might have to drag Jason out of bed," Parker told Chase. "I haven't seen the likes of him since last night."

"That boy had you both beat by an hour. He ate and went exploring, taking all of his cameras with him." Ethel grabbed Parker's finished plate and took it to the sink.

"Wow, Jason up early? He's the one who's always late." Parker stood, pushed his chair in and ruffled Chase's hair. "I guess we'll meet you out there."

Chase nodded as he continued to chew the mouthful of his breakfast. He raised his fork as Parker placed his hat on his head and walked out the front door.

The country here was so different. The greens were greener, the trees older, taller, and had bigger leaves. His eyes could see for miles without the dry desert dust fogging his view. The farming land patterned the fields like an artist's canvas. Perfect rows of crops. He imagined it to be more of a fairytale land than somewhere humans would live. What would Blossom think about seeing this much green grass in one place?

Parker's feet followed a walkway, unaware of where it would lead him. His body felt free and refreshed after being confined to a plane and a small cottage. The air was damp and warmer than the night before.

The path led to an enormous building. It was more wide than tall. Curious, he walked in. Amazed at the fencing that edged a covered arena, he ran a finger over it to make sure it was real. Each panel was carved into a decorative painted white wood. One side of the area had bleachers for spectators, the other side for other horses with their riders to warm up before entering the main arena. The opening in the front had tables, chairs and a food vender that was currently closed.

In the main arena, there was a female rider. The rider kept her horse in a perfect form. Her saddle was so small. He cringed, his nose wrinkling at the thought of sitting on it. There was no way she could possibly stay on that little flap of leather if her horse bolted or bucked. Her long black boots rose to her knees, and her gloved hands stayed in front of the horse's withers, unmoved.

A light classical music played in the background and the horse seemed to match every beat perfectly, as if he and his rider were dancing. Blossom could do this with some practice, but making her trot so evenly, he wasn't so sure. The dark brown horse was mesmerizing as he pranced around, his rhythm perfect.

"I see you arrived safely," the rider said, stopping her horse in the middle of the arena.

A little shocked as a prickle of embarrassment trickled down his spine, he looked around to see who she was talking to. Unfortunately, he was the only other person in the building. "Uh. Yes. Thank you?" Parker adjusted his hat, landing it back to the exact spot it sat before on his head.

Her blue eyes stared at him. The chill in the air caused a redness to her nose and checks. Her dark hair gelled perfectly into a ballerina bun on the top of her head. He had never seen such an image. She was like a glass doll, perfect features all around. She was beautiful. A flutter tickled inside of him.

"I'm Charlotte."

"Parker." He tipped his hat.

"Yes, I know."

Parker scratched the back of his neck as the heat of embarrassment rose in to his head and caused a quick dizzy spell. "I, uh. Hope it's okay, I came in here? It's nice. Fancy."

The sapphire in her eyes darkened.

"Sorry?" he questioned, as he lifted an eyebrow.

"No. It is quite all right." She shifted in her saddle. The horse walked up closer to the fence edge where Parker stood. "Do you want to ride?"

Parker ran his tongue over his top teeth. "I don't mean to offend, but would it be in one of those?" He pointed at the saddle under her behind, which he imagined being a delightful view.

Charlotte laughed. "Did you bring one of your American saddles?"

Cursing under his breath at Chase, he rubbed the stubble on his jawline. "No."

"Well, then, Sir Cowboy, it is an English saddle or none at all." A smile rose on her lips as she watched the handsome man in front of her struggle. He shifted from one boot stance to the other. She bit down on her bottom lips as she admired him in person. She knew it would hurt his pride to sit in anything other than his western hunk of leather. Charlotte had watched their channel, seen every episode, and she knew Parker was the broody one, and proud of his cowboy heritage. Something about that fascinated her.

Parker swallowed, forcing a hard lump of awkward feelings that had formed in his throat. He scuffed his boot against the soft ground. "I guess I could look at the horses you have available."

"Very well. Do you mind meeting me over there," she pointed to the other side of the arena, "and bringing my step inside?"

A small huff escaped Parker's mouth.

"Do you mock me, sir?"

"No," his face reddened, "I just didn't see why you would need help on or off."

With that, Charlotte gently placed her reins on her horse's neck, put both her gloved hands right in front of her saddle, and kicked both her legs out in a straight line behind her. Gracefully, she landed on the ground next to her horse, with a small puff of dirt at her feet. "I don't *need* the step. It's just an aide."

Parker stood there, his eyes wide, at the gate, still holding the step he had yet to bring into the arena. He watched her thin feminine frame lead the tall gelding out of the fence he was now holding open. He admired her backend as she walked out. In her form fitting skin-tight breeches, it was hard to miss. Maybe Chase was right. The yoga pants were kind of nice.

"If you wouldn't mind. I could use your help with my boots."

Pushing the gate closed, he raised an eyebrow. Help with her boots? Was she unable to take off her own shoes? If everyone here needed help with their boots and mounting, what could they do? What had he walked into?'

She walked the gelding out a side door; it opened into an enclosed barn. Smells of horses, leather, pine shaving and musk intoxicated Parker's senses. The horses' hooves clicked and clanged over the cobblestones. Stall doors lined both sides to the right. To his left open stalls for tacking, washing, and storing items. A glass chandelier hung from the middle, lighting the barn in a warmth. The top half of the stalls had a twisted and shaped iron decoration, while a dark amber wood lined the bottom half.

Most of the stalls contained well-groomed, enormous, spoiled horses. He assumed they were warm-bloods. "I have never seen such a beautiful barn."

"Well, you wouldn't know where you are from, would you?"

"Excuse me?"

"Sorry," she apologized. "I didn't mean for that to come out as snarky." She unbuckled the one cinch that held her saddle to her horse. "If you wouldn't mind." She nodded her head toward the black flap of leather she called a saddle.

Parker slid one arm under, gently lifting it off the back of her horse. He almost laughed at the weightless effort it took. Someone had pampered this woman. *She wouldn't last a day on the ranch*, he thought.

"It goes there," Charlotte pointed behind them. "In that open door, any open holder will work. That is my own personal room."

Following her directions, he walked into the smell of leather and horse. A room bigger than his bedroom at home. It was like walking into a tack store: bridles, saddles, blankets, grooming items of every shape and form. He set the saddle neatly onto an open rack, smoothing it out the best he knew how. He cocked his head to the side, hoping it was sitting correctly.

Turning to walk out, he caught her watching him. A faint pink surfaced on her cheeks. "Thank you." She rubbed her forehead and walked back to her horse.

Parker helped brush the dark brown gelding down, and they walked him back to a stall that was kept cleaner than his own room. "These horses are spoiled. Ours back home wouldn't know what to do in something this fancy."

Charlotte laughed. "We have some quarter horses here. They are kept on the other side of the barn."

"Oh, I see. Our American breeds are not good enough for this side, huh?"

"No." Charlotte chuckled. "The barn master just likes to keep them stabled by breed." Parker wasn't as broody in person as he seemed on camera. She liked this witty version of him.

She led Parker down yet another wing of the stable. It, too, was another inside barn full of spoiled horses. This side held smaller stouter horses. A smile grew on Parker's face. He knew even though these were quarter horses, the price tag on the breeding could buy a house.

"Wow, this place. It is breathtaking."

"Take your pick." Charlotte twirled a wrist and waved it along the line of doors. "All of them are quite lovely. Might I suggest this stallion down this way?"

Gladly, he followed her framed behind. "This one was shipped from the King Ranch in Texas." She stopped in front of the iron barns. Watching, waiting for his reaction.

Parker peeked in. Inside stood a buckskin stallion that looked like he had been on steroids his whole life. His golden coat shone in the light and his black mane looked as though it was brushed and conditioned daily. His tiny head encased large, kind eyes. "Gorgeous."

"I could use some help with my boots still, if you wouldn't mind? I'm late for a meeting. Maybe we could ride the stallion tomorrow?"

"Yeah, sure. That would be great." Parker's shoulders drooped in disappointment, but only for a moment.

Again, he followed her gladly. Tipping his hat to contain his enjoyment and cover the smile on his face, as he followed her back to her personal tack room. She sat down on a bench she held out one of her legs.

Lifting his hat to scratch an itch that wasn't there, he paused. Parker grabbed the boot, expecting it to come off with ease, it didn't budge. He pulled harder, almost pulling the lady off her seat. "Shoot, I'm sorry." Her rump half flew off the bench as her fingers scraped to hold on.

"If you grab the heel, push it forward first. It will help," Charlotte suggested. A grin rolled over her lips watching the handsome American cowboy try to take off her boot. His touch was warm even through the thin leather. Heat fogged her thoughts. She bit her lip, doing her best to not let him see her enjoyment.

Not without a tremendous effort, he did as she asked. A few beads of sweat rolled down his back and under the brim of his hat. He had never had to work so hard to get a pair of boots off in his life. "I don't know why you would want to go through that every time. You might want to look into getting some new boots." He lifted his hat with his right hand and wiped his left forearm over his damp brow.

Charlotte laughed. "I do have a pair with zippers, but these are more comfortable." She smiled at him. She was pretty. His body responded, and he quickly glanced away. The urge to pull her closer to him grew stronger. Why was he feeling this way? It'd been too long since he let a woman so attractive get this close to him.

They both turned to the sound of foots steps on the cobblestone hallway. A man dressed in a suit approached them down the aisle. As he traveled, he carried his hands behind him. He stopped in front of them, a little out of breath. He bowed at the waist. "Your Highness. You are expected for tea."

Parker's eyebrows furrowed. "Your Highness?" he whispered. How had he been so stupid? Was he supposed to bow? Instead, he just stood there like an ignorant chum.

"Yes. Princess Charlotte. Daughter of King Edward the third," the suited man spat out.

Charlotte glanced over at him, a wicked gleam in her blue eyes, and curtsied. "Until next time, Cowboy."

When she walked off, he watched the ground. Cursing himself for not realizing he had been talking to royalty the entire time. How could he have not known? She had played him, stringing him along like a fish on an empty hook.

The man in the suit gave Parker a smug look, his eyes rolled up and down. One of his eyes twitched. Parker stood taller, ready to fight back with whatever this guy threw at him. He could easily take this suited snob. Instead, he looked Parker up and down once more, huffed, turned on his heels and headed after the Princess.

Once they both had left, Parker walked back to the buckskin, who was chewing his hay blissfully. His gigantic horse eyes were in a dreamy state as he ground his molars over the roughage. "Why didn't you tell me that was the princess? Us Americans got to watch out for one another."

The stallion's left ear moved to acknowledge that he heard Parker, but only kept chewing. Parker rubbed his temples under his hat. He knew the difference in time zones was going to hit him like a bag of sand in a few days. He could feel it coming.

"Nice horses," Chase said as he walked up to Parker, who was still rubbing his pounding head.

Parker's heart skipped a few beats at Chase's interruption. "Yeah. I wouldn't be able to afford one in my lifetime."

"I wouldn't be so sure of that. Our videos could get us there." Chase gestured with his hands to their surroundings as he spun around. "It got us to this. So, what has your panties in a jumble?"

"I go out to get some fresh air, and then I happen to find myself in this oversized horse mansion." Parker gestured to their surroundings. "Unknown to me, the princess is riding her horse in the arena. I smarted off to her a few times. I wasn't completely rude, but if I had known she was who she was, I would have acted differently."

Chase bellowed over in laughter. His hands made their way to his knees. "You are always making the wrong impression. Oh, shoot, that is just too good. Was she pretty?"

Parker's left eyebrow lifted. His lips pressed into a thin line.

"That good, huh?"

"Yeah. That good."

The guys headed out of the barn. "Unfortunately, she is off limits." Chase laughed again. "Only you, my man. Only you."

"Hey! There you guys are," Jason said as Chase closed the door to the barn. "I have been taking shots around the grounds. This place is incredible. I have some ideas for great videos, too."

"Parker here," Chase said, thumbing at his friend. "Already put a good word in with the princess."

"Which one? There are two of them," Jason informed them.

"Two?" Parker and Chase both said at the same time.

"Yeah." Jason adjusted his camera strap over his arm. "The older one is engaged to some prince from a far-off land, you know, the gig. The younger one is the one who invited us here. She's fascinated with the American cowboy."

"So, which one did you meet, Parker?" Chase asked.

"Well, I didn't ask which princess she was." Parker shuffled his boots on the ground. "I had just found out after I had not treated her princess-like, remember?"

"Her name, numb skull. What is her name? Or did you not get that, either?" Chase rolled his eyes.

"Charlotte," Parker said under his breath.

"That's the younger one," Jason said.

"Figures he would offend the one we have to spend the next month with." Chase sighed and slapped Parker on the back. A hallow thud followed.

"Come on." Jason signaled for them to follow him. "I'll introduce you to David. He's assigned to help us while we are here. He's cool. You'll like him."

Jason led Parker and Chase about half a mile away from the barn. A wide, fast-moving river ran along the edge of a waist-high white fence. A towering canopy of trees created a dark, cool cover over the flowing water. On the other side stood a man with a fishing rod. As they neared, he waved. "Cheers friends."

"David, meet Parker and Chase." Jason smiled at his two American friends. "They were in the barn checking out the horses."

"How did you find it? Was it to your liking?" David asked, reeling up his line.

"I've seen nothing like it," Parker said.

"Great. Great. I'm here to help you lads with whatever you might need, want, and so on. We have a daily schedule to work with, since you'll be meeting often with the Princess. I'll keep you up to date on any appointments."

"Can I ask for anything?" Chase teased.

"Yes. I've been instructed to do my best to meet all your needs, whatever they might be." David gave a fake cheesy grin.

"We are going to need some western saddles." Parker narrowed his eyes at Chase.

"Oh dear. The ones we have in the barn won't suffice?" David asked.

"Have you seen the saddles in the barn?" Parker pointed behind him.

"Come on, Park, they can't be all that bad," Chase said.

"A little leather flap and an iron oval-like shape for our enormous feet?" Parker eyed Chase. "And one little strap and a buckle for a cinch."

"I might pay money to see you ride this leather flap," Chase teased.

Parker pulled off his hat and fingered the inside rim. "I might want to punch you right now."

Lifting his fists, Chase widened his stance. "Bring it buddy."

"Now, now, gentlemen. Let's not get too hasty here," David said, trying to ease the tension between the cowboys. "Let's talk about our schedule tomorrow instead?" David's voice cracked.

Parker put his hat back on his head. "It was all just in fun and games, David. You know that, right?" He winked at Chase. Still wanting deep down to punch his friend for talking him out of leaving his saddle at home.

"Well, you cowboys are just so rough sometimes," David said under his breath. "Besides the point, tomorrow, the princess has asked you all to join her on a fox hunt."

"To be clear, which princess?" Chase asked.

"I believe they will both be in attendance," David said.

"And they expect us to ride the leather flap?" Parker's eyebrow lifted.

"Well, yes sir, it's… Well, unfortunately, all we have at the moment." David's grip tightened on a clipboard he held. "I will put in a request to get your western saddles, but it may take a few days."

Parker sighed. Chase laughed. "Oh, just you wait until you see what you'll be riding in." Parker pushed a finger into Chase's shoulder, pushing him back a little.

"I'll have your riding gear set in your rooms. And you'll need to be ready promptly at nine," David said. "You gentlemen enjoy the rest of your evening and please, don't hesitate to call if you need me. Jason has my number."

The three of them walked back to their cottage. Ethel was in the kitchen finishing their dinner. The aroma of freshly baked bread lingered in the small house. "Hope your first day was well spent?" she inquired.

"It was nice and relaxing," Parker replied. "What's for dinner?"

"Lasagna Bolognese and sliced bread."

"Wow, first class service here," Chase said. He sat on the couch in front of the fireplace and kicked up his feet, still inside his boots, onto the coffee table. He placed his hat over his face and leaned his head back.

"Chase, it might be nice for the furniture if you to take your boots off at least?" Parker suggested.

Without even taking the hat off his face, Chase lifted a boot, holding it in the air. "Help a poor cowboy out?"

"Are you kidding me, man?"

Lifting his hat, Chase batted his eyes. "Please?"

"Only because it's rude. And I'm embarrassed by your house manners." Parker walked over and yanked the boot off his friend. "This is the second time today I pulled someone else's boots off."

The hat came up again. "Who else uses you to take their boots off? I'm offended you offered this service to another."

With a swift throw, the boot went flying into his owner.

"Ouch!" Chase said. "You're such a jerk, Parker."

"Good, next time take your own boots off."

Parker left the family room and went to his room. Neatly folded at every crease was a button-down polo and elastic breeches. Next to the dresser was a pair of long, black, knee-high boots and a top hat. "You've got to be kidding me. There is no way in hell I'm wearing this garbage." He grabbed the pile and set them in the corner, along with the boots. He wanted to place it all in the trash-can, but didn't, as he didn't want to offend his hosts.

CHAPTER 5 THE FOX HUNT

The next morning, the three guys walked over to the barn. There were at least thirty horses and riders out front. Some mounted, some not. Men in white leggings, red or black coat jackets, and top hats were not something Parker or Chase wanted to be part of. One man stood holding a leash with several English Foxhounds, white, brown, and spotted. Their long ears dragged on the ground as they sniffed and howled, pulling on the leashes.

"Why are all these guys dressed like pansies?" Chase whispered to Parker.

"I'm just glad you didn't walk out this morning dressed like one."

"Did you get that weird pile, too?"

"Yeah. I didn't want to ask if you did. I was so embarrassed to even admit I touched them." Chase straightened up as one of the mounted men glared at the two cowboys. His eyes rolled up and down at the boots and jeans they wore in disgust.

David found the three Americans easily. Their cowboys' hats versus the black top hats made them stick out. "You, um, boys weren't happy with the traditional hunter's outfits?"

Chase laughed. Parker said nothing.

"They aren't exactly what we are used to," Jason added.

"Noted." David nodded. "If you gentlemen would step into the barn, I believe they have a couple of mounts ready for you."

Sure enough, there were three horses saddled, each held by a groomsman. "These will be your mounts today. We season all these horses before they go on hunting trips, so there shouldn't be any serious issues. The three of you are experienced riders." David eyed them. "Right?"

"Yes," Parker replied. He adjusted his hat, annoyed he was being forced to ride in the small piece of leather.

"They assigned each of you a groomsman. They will help you further. Please enjoy yourselves today," David said. He placed his hands together in front of himself, and with a slight bow, he left.

Chase picked the tall black gelding. Forcing his leg past its stretch point, he barely managed to get his large boot into the iron stirrup with a minor force. He grabbed the front of the saddle and attempted to hoist himself up, as he did, his blue jeans split. A loud ripping of the fabric caused every head to turn. The tear traveled up from the side of his crotch, following his buttocks.

Red faced, and wide eyes, Chase paused. He reached back to feel the gaping hole on his backside. "You've got to be kidding me."

"Uh sir," the young lad next to him said. "Your pants just..." The boy pointed.

Ignoring the boy, Chase continued to pull himself up. His large stature rolled the saddle to the side of the horse. He hobbled backward, almost falling to his rear. "What the hell!"

Parker laughed so hard he almost couldn't control himself. "I told you! Worthless," he said between breaths.

The boy adjusted the cinch and saddle. "If I may, sir?" He held his hands together and bent over, signaling for Chase to step inside his cupped hands.

An eyebrow rose over Chase's baby blues. Shaking his head vigorously in disbelief. "You're kidding right now, right?"

"No, sir. This is how it is done," the groom said.

More laughter escaped from Parker and Jason. Chase looked over at them, only able to blink a few times. He opened his mouth to say something and decided to just comply.

Jason and Parker allowed their grooms to help them mount. They didn't want to repeat Chase's mistake. Once atop their horses, their grooms led them out to join the other riders. Parker shook his head. He had a knot in his stomach because of the unstable saddle beneath him.

As the cowboys entered the clearing, the loud chatter of men stopped. The seasoned hunt-riders stared at the strange blue jeans, brown leathered boot men in cowboy hats. "Clearly, they don't belong here," one of them blurted out.

"Fellow riders," one of them said. He wore a gold embellished coat, standing out in rank over the other men. "Let's welcome our American cowboy stars.

Chase, Parker, and Jason. Shall we show them how the first original *real* men rode?"

The group of them cheered. The dogs howled with excitement.

"Now, boys, is that any way to treat our guests?" a female voice said. She sat sidesaddle on a white horse. Ruffles of velvety red material folded over her legs, only her one foot visible. A gold embellishment matching the man who just spoke trimmed over the edges of the wrinkled material.

Proudly, she walked her horse closer and stopped next to Chase. Her smile directed at the handsome cowboy. Chase blushed. "I am Princess Mary." She lifted her white gloved hand toward the man who last spoke. "This is my fiancé, Prince Alexander." The prince puffed his chest slightly. His grin matched the snarky attire.

Mary nodded to Parker. He saw a resemblance between her and her sister in their sapphire eyes, but Mary's hair differed in color, her blonde locks flowed behind her like rays of sunshine. "My sister is running a little behind. We leave when she arrives."

"This saddle hurts my butt," Chase leaned over to tell Parker.

Chuckling, Parker looked down to hide his laughter under the brim of his hat. He shook his head back and forth, feeling naked on top of the tiny piece of leather between his legs. The red horse underneath him shook her neck, her body shuttered under him, and he grabbed a hold of her mane to steady the uncomfortable feeling.

Surprised from the shivering horse he, jumped a little to a voice behind him. "We meet again, Cowboy."

Lifting his gaze from the mane of his horse, Parker looked up to meet the blue eyes of the princess he had met yesterday. Charlotte. She was more beautiful in the sun's light. She had once again tied her brown hair into a tight bun. Unlike her sister, she wore breeches like the men and straddled a leg on each side of the horse. She bit on her lip, waiting for him to respond.

Parker struggled to find something to say. His thoughts raced with thousands of ideas, but they only collided with one another. He stared at the lip under her white teeth, imaging what they would be like to kiss. He hadn't thought about a woman like this since—Briel. His heart saddened, a little even at the thought of her name. A dry lump formed in his throat, furthering his ability to say anything.

"Excuse my friend," Chase said, thumping Parker on his bicep. "I think he's still in shock that he has to sit upon this hideous nothing of a saddle." Chase held out his hand. "I'm Chase."

"Charlotte," the princess said, nodding, but not taking his hand.

"Are you ready, sister?" Mary asked. "I still can't believe father let you get away with riding the hunt in men's trousers."

Charlotte looked back once at Parker, who still sat there speechless. He watched her and her sister ride their horses to the front of the herd of riders. A few of them shaking heads in disgust and turning up their noses.

"You imbecile. Get her out of your head. There is no way you and her can ever work," Chase told his friend. "You could have any woman you wanted and you pick the untouchable one." Chase lifted his hat and ran his free hand through his hair.

"I didn't say I was interested." Parker shook his head in denial.

"I just watched you. You got it bad." Chase placed the hat back on his blond hair.

Parker looked back at Jason. He shrugged, his lips pressed together, as he nodded in agreement with Chase.

A horn sounded, and the riders took off. The three cowboy's horses lunged into a trot, startling them before they were ready. All of them leaned forward to balance their bodies from falling. The hound dog's leashes were released, and they paced ahead, howling into the air. Parker winced as the leather strap that connected under the saddle to the iron his boot was in pinched his leg.

The horses ahead of them broke into a canter, following the hounds. The three cowboys reined back to observe, slowing their horses. They were unsure of what to expect. The dogs ran for a good mile before ducking into a wooded forest. Thankfully, they followed along a road, and the tree branches were high enough not to knock off their hats.

After about twenty minutes, just as Parker sort of got used to the foreign saddle underneath of him, the dogs went berserk. The horn sounded again, and the riders took off through an unmarked path into the thick of the trees. Keeping one hand on his hat and the other on the reins, Parker struggled to stay on. Bobbing up and down on the odd saddle, he tried to slow his excited horse. The red mare pulled at the bit, urging to race forward with the rest of the horses.

"Yeehaw!" Chase yelled, waving his hat in the wind like a crazy man as he passed. Jason was right on his heels, his eyes wide, highlighting a pale face as he rode by. His white knuckles gripped his reins and hung on for life. The other hand was tangled in mane as he muscled the horse to slow down.

Holding tight, Parker still reined his mare back. She fought him to keep up with the others. The knot in his stomach still lingered. He stayed stiff and uncomfortable in the saddle, and didn't want any obstacles suddenly jumping out at him at a high speed.

The hunters in front of him dodged low branches. Jumped over fallen tree trunks and plowed through low brush. It impressed Parker with the skills the riders had to have to stay with the quick movements of their horses. Even knowing he was a confident rider, he still felt unsure. He had ridden since before he could walk, so he had to trust himself. He loosened the reins, and the anxious mare lunged forward, taking advantage of the loosening on her bit. She leaped into the air, soaring like a butterfly flying over the fallen logs. Parker stayed with her, leaning over her powerful neck muscles.

He could hear the dogs baying louder, longer, and more aggressively. Parker pulled his mare to a stop as he reached the swarm of shouting hunters surrounding a tree. He found Chase and Jason hanging in the back.

"This is comical. These guys are so into this," Chase said.

"It might be something like roping a cow back home," Jason added.

Parker nodded.

"What took you so long?" Chase eyed Parker.

"I just wanted to hold back and enjoy the view, I guess."

"See anything good?" Chase's eyebrow lifted and down.

"Not really." Parker patted his mare's neck. Her ribcage still heaved in and out from her gallop to catch up. "I do like this horse. Very athletic. I'm not sure Blossom could have jumped like that."

"That's because we bred her for jumping." Charlotte rode up next to the three cowboys. Bringing her big gelding next to Parker's red mare. "You boys rode well."

"Thank you," Chase said, his flirty smile bigger than normal. "What do they do with the fox when they catch it?"

"In the past, they would have skinned it, used it as decretive clothing. These days, we trap it and re-release it for another hunt. It's more for the thrill."

The brown gelding Charlotte sat upon pawed the ground. He shifted to his opposite hind leg; she steadied him. "That's a spirted horse," Chase added, impressed she could handle such a large creature.

"I like them that way." She winked. "Parker, would you ride back with me?"

His brown eyes surfaced from the rim of his hat to meet her sapphires. "Me?" He pointed to his chest. He glanced quickly at Chase. His friend lifted one eyebrow, encouraging Parker to take the offer with caution.

"Yes. Your name is Parker, isn't?" she teased.

A pink warmth surfaced over his sun-kissed skin. He lifted his hat and scratched his head. Her eyes never left the good-looking cowboy in front of her. Her confidence was almost intimidating, but something about it drove Parker into a madness. Inside of him screamed to say yes. Yet, he knew he shouldn't let his attraction to her grow. There was no chance a princess could have feelings for a cowboy from Arizona. Not one who carried a lot of baggage.

Just one ride wouldn't hurt. He was strong enough to fight any small feelings. Besides, those feelings were only surfacing. They would be easy to shove away. Nodding, he accepted. "I would love to ride with you. Anywhere you have in mind?" He glanced at Chase, his eyes searching for any signs of disapproval. Chase raised both eyebrows and gave his friend a quaint smile.

Charlotte looked over her shoulder at her sister and future brother-in-law. They were distracted by the fox, the barking hounds and the other hunters, who were all shouting in excitement. "Hurry this way." She pointed to Chase and Jason. "You will tell them I felt faint and Mr. Parker has escorted me home."

"Yes, ma'am." Chase tipped his black cowboy hat.

The princess reined the big gelding away from the other two cowboys, and Parker followed. She started at a trot, then into a canter. "Keep her collected if you can. There are some big jumps ahead."

A prickle of fear caused Parker to doubt himself. He didn't know the horse that well, nor was he comfortable in the small saddle, and now the pressure was on him to impress a beautiful princess.

The princess swayed between trees. Parker's horse followed close behind. Branches of trees swished past him, scratching his bare arms. Luckily, the brim of his hat protected his face.

The brown gelding quickly rocked back on his haunches and launched into the air over a small creek. Not expecting his horse to do the same, Parker lost his balance. The mare jumped over the watery path. Parker held on for his life at her side, attached like an adolescent monkey to its mother. His right leg hung over her back and his arms clutched around her neck.

Charlotte pulled her mount to a halt. "Are you alright?" She watched the muscles in his forearms strain, the veins popping out through the skin as he pulled himself upright again. "What happened?"

"I wasn't ready for her to jump like that. She rode so close to your gelding, and I couldn't see what was ahead."

"Are you ok to continue? It's not much farther."

"Yeah. I'm good." They kicked the horses into a canter. The trees in the forest slowly spread apart as they came to an opening. In the middle of the clearing stood a crumbling building. No evidence of a roof existed and only the stones that made the outer rim remained, uneven and unfinished.

Dismounting in front of him, Charlotte bent over to adjust her boot. Parker quickly looked away, as he found his eyes wandering. He followed suit and led his horse next to hers. "I used to come here as a girl. To escape my lessons. And get away from the politics."

"What was it before it became shambles?"

"There are stories that it once belonged to a witch. They burned her inside, along with everything she owned. They say it's haunted." She smiled, her blue eyes sparkling. "But we know that isn't true. That is just something the children have told each other."

She tied her horse to a post. "There was a man who worked his whole life as a slave. His master promised he could earn his freedom if he worked hard and never complained. He fell in love and to show her the feelings of his heart, he built this house with his own hands, one stone at a time."

Charlotte walked into what would have been the inside of the small home. She traced her fingers along the stones. They were uneven and in ruins, yet still standing. Parker followed her. She turned a corner and stopped in a small area that may have been a bedroom, but it was hard to tell with the missing pieces. She bent down, pushed a rock from the wall, and pulled out an old rope. "The actual story is that the man was a cowboy who belonged to a faraway land. He never finished building the house, because they sent him back. So, the house stayed, fading until it became what it is today."

"And that was his rope?" Parker asked, following her out of the open walls.

"No." Charlotte laughed. "This one is mine. I found it at a trade fair. I'm not very good. I was hoping you could teach me. She twirled the rope over her head and threw it at an old hay bale. Two sticks stuck out of the end of the ratty bale. Parker caulked his head to one side. He assumed it was supposed to resemble a cow. Charlotte twirled the rope, threw it, and missed.

"Can I show you?" Parker asked.

The princess held the rope out to him as he took it, their fingers brushed past each other. Soft. Warm. His need to hold her and press her lips against his own boiled inside of him.

"Flatten the hand out, like it's pointing to where you want it to go, right as the circle hits the top of the twirl." He demonstrated. The rope glided over him effortlessly. "When you're ready, you release." The rope circled over both sticks and he pulled tight, causing one of them to pop out of place. "Then you dally." He pretended to wrap his rope around the saddle horn that wasn't there.

Charlotte's face reddened, and her eyes shot to the ground. He knew he had impressed her. His heart fluttered. Walking over to replace the stick, he loosened the rope. He showed her again. He wanted to do it a hundred more times, just so he could watch her reaction. Keeping them in this moment forever.

"Can I try?" she asked. Taking the rope, Charlotte positioned herself as he had shown. She attempted to circle the rope, but failed to do it as he had done.

"Would you be okay if I helped you?" Parker winced. The pain of watching her try so hard was almost painful.

She nodded. He walked up behind her. Wrapping his arms around her shoulders, his body tensed. Her compact frame fit perfectly into his own. Her warm curves, exciting every piece of him. Telling himself to relax, he took a few deep inhales. This only made it worst. Her hair smelled of flowers and honey. Parker had to force his eyes to focus instead of wanting to roll back in his head. He placed his arm over hers, guiding her through the motion, around and around. "Let it go flat at the top, point and release."

With his help, the rope caught the branches. The princess jumped with excitement and her body moved against his. His eyes widened as his desires escalated.

Quickly, Parker released his arms and backed away, adjusting to hide his red face.

"I can't believe that little hand motion is all it takes."

"Well, it takes some practice. You'll want to move out of the shoulder and not the elbow to get a good swing."

Parker watched her. She was graceful, taught to carry herself as a royal. She was confident. Her eyes bore into his as she walked close, never leaving contact. His heart pounded as she neared, betraying him as the warmth almost blinded him.

Stopping close enough for their lips to touch, she reached up and pulled off his hat. "I have been watching you for a long time." He could feel the movement of her lips almost against his own, breath warm on his face. Afraid to break a rule, or offend her, he resisted the urge to pull her into a fierce kiss. Her scent wafted over him. Intoxicating.

She placed his hat on top of her brown hair. Her hair draped over her shoulders, windblown, but still beautiful. "I want you to show me how to be a cowgirl. I want my own hat, a pair of those sexy dirt caked boots, and tight blue jeans." She traced his bottom lip with her pointer finger. The wind blew the scent of flowers and honey, and his knees threatened to wobble. Imagining her as she described, his body shivered, betraying him. Spots blurred his vision as he fought to keep his composure. The heat was too much. It took every ounce of strength he had to stay standing.

Parker swallowed, forcing the large lump of nerves that had formed. Too dry to move, it only bopped up and down in this throat. "Okay." Was all he could manage with a voice crack. Still unsure how to react to a royal that was invading his personal bubble, he remained a statue. Frozen.

Charlotte brought her hand to his face and cupped the side of his masculine jawline. She rubbed her thumb over his dark stubble. Her eyes narrowed, studying him. He waited for any sign of rejection. "What do I have to do to get you to kiss me? Are all of you American cowboys so stiff?"

Parker blinked several times. Was this really happening? He wasn't sure if all of this was just one giant nightmare he could wake up from. Briel was the last person he had kissed. It had been a few years. Would he even remember how? He knew he needed to move on, but he wanted this. It's why he had agreed to the videos. They allowed him to drown in their work. Stay busy and forget he could have feelings. He placed a hand over hers. The warmth of it under his fingertips, sparking something inside of him. He pushed whatever it was away and brought her hand down.

The shine on her face dampened. Her brows angered slightly with the rejection. "You don't want to kiss me?" The whisper came out sharp. Her bold moves, not expecting rejection.

"No. I mean. Yes. I just, I don't…" Parker growled at himself.

"You don't like girls?" She held her hand over her mouth. "I'm so sorry. I'm so embarrassed. I just assumed. I should have known. I am so sorry!" She paced in a circle, his hat still on her head.

"What? No! I like women."

"You do?" Charlotte's shoulder slumped slightly. She bit her lip as a wave of relief washed over her.

"Yes, I most definitely do. I just had a... My last relationship went bad, and I haven't been able to let myself move on. I need to. It's just hard." He ran his fingers through his dark greasy hair.

Charlotte grabbed his hands and held them in hers. "I understand in a way. For a long time, I couldn't let happiness return after my mother's death. I know it is not quite the same. And I'm not trying to compare. However, you lost her, it's okay. Maybe I could help you forget?"

His chocolate brown eyes met hers. "Yeah, I would like that." He had caved. His body overpowered his mind.

She reached up to pull the hat off her head and place it back on his, but he stopped her. "No. Keep it. I have another. It looks good on you."

"Really?"

Parker nodded. Charlotte stood up on her tippy-toes and kissed his cheek. Her lips were so soft. He kicked himself for not taking her up on the invitation earlier. It just needed it to be the right moment. Whatever that meant. He wanted it to mean something. Someone to love him for him. Not because he was famous on social media, or because a spoiled princess took whatever she wanted. With her, he knew it could not last. He couldn't let his heart get tangled in that kind of relationship again.

They rode the horses back to the castle grounds. Most of the fox hunters had left. Only Mary and the prince remained. When they walked up, she was yelling at whoever got in her way. "I can't believe you would just let her take off! What if she's hurt? My little sister is the princess, for heaven's sakes!"

"Mary," Charlotte said, as her sister whipped her head around. "I'm quite fine. I made sure I had an escort." She looked back at Parker, who was dismounting his horse.

"You were alone? With him?" Mary stormed over to Parker. Her footsteps pounded the ground. She stopped right in front of his face. What was with these princesses and their no space boundaries? She pushed a finger into his hard chest. He felt the tip of her fingernail digging into his skin, even through his shirt. "If you laid even one hair on my sister's head, you will regret it!"

Both of his hands came up in surrender. "I didn't touch her."

"Good! Keep it that way!" Mary spun around to her sister. "And you, I'll make sure you have an escort from now on while the American cowboys are here. And what is that ridiculous hat?"

Charlotte's face grew redder than a beet. Her eyes narrowed and her fist clenched together. "You're not my mother!" She grabbed her gelding's mane, swung her leg over his back, and spun him in a pivot, kicking him violently into a gallop. The dust from the horses' hooves hung in the air behind her.

Parker didn't think twice. He also swung a leg over and was in a gallop after the princess in a matter of seconds. "Stop!" Mary yelled after the two of them. "Someone, follow them!" Her voice boomed with anger and her arm shook as she pointed in their direction.

Pointing to his chest, Chase looked around for anyone else. There was no one. What had he walked into? He had hoped to turn around and leave before they noticed he had walked up, but he was too late.

"No. Not you," Mary spit out, growling out a scream afterward. She planted her feet, scowled at her fiancé, and stomped toward the castle.

"That was awkward," Jason told Chase, walking up next to him chewing on a cheese stick.

"You're telling me." Chase rubbed at his chin. "Let's go see if Ethel has made something to eat."

"Good idea."

***

Running through the open countryside gave Parker a sense of freedom. A feeling he missed from back home. The red mare under him had a long stride, but she was no match for the princess, still wearing his hat in front of him. Her dark brown hair flowing like a wave underneath it.

Parker followed her until the horses slowed. Parker urged his mare a little more so she could catch up. Charlotte's face was plastered with salty tracks. Her eyes were red and puffy from tears.

"Charlotte, are you okay? Did you want to talk about it?"

She huffed once, sniffing. "She thinks she can take my mother's place. No one can ever replace my mum."

"No. You're right."

"She gets the throne. She inherits everything. And what do I get? To be bossed around by her?" Charlotte pulled the brown gelding to a halt and dismounted him. "I don't want to be the one who is second to her."

"I don't think you have to. Right?" He dismounted. "Do you?" Parker walked up next to her. She stood looking out over an edge. Jagged rocks lined the bottom of the cliff side where the ocean sent its waves to end a wave cycle. Beautiful. A repeat of the same wave, yet each one was so unique when it crashed with the rocks to create a deadly splash.

The princess grabbed onto his forearm, noticing the hard muscle that warmed her icy hand. "Will you teach me, so I can leave here with you?"

"Back to America?"

"Yes. She will marry Alexander. She'll be crowned queen, and I will either be married off to unite other kingdoms to some pompous I've never met. Or continue to rebel and cause harm to my family name."

"Are you normally a troublemaker?" Parker scratched his eyebrow, wondering what he had gotten himself into.

Charlotte laughed. She bent down, picked up a rock, and threw it over the edge. "Wouldn't you want to leave?"

"Well, I... It seems nice here." Parker shrugged. "The stable has a lot of nice horses."

"Stuffy tea parties, prissy ball gowns, fake smiles. Is that something you want?" Charlotte was now staring into Parker's brown eyes. The blue of hers darker under his hat. "Or would you want to ride, rope, run free, and do what your heart pleaded for?"

"I suppose the latter. But I've never been one for crowds, or tea." Parker's nose wrinkled at the thought.

"Exactly," she said, folding her arms over her chest. "I'm going to ask you again. And you're going to have to make a quick decision, because my sister more than likely has the army on their way to bring me back to my prison cell they call my bedroom."

"Okay?" Parker questioned, moving a little closer to her. His heart pounding a little harder with anticipation.

"I want you to kiss me, and if there is any sort of spark, take me with you to America."

Parker cleared his throat and rubbed the back of his neck that instantly had gone hot. "Isn't a kiss something that's shared between two people who have, uh, known each other for a while? Who want a relationship?"

"Stop being so romantic." Charlotte batted his chest. "I know you think I'm attractive. I see the way act around me. You get hot, blush and squirm around in your own skin. And why the hell do you think I wanted you here? It wasn't because you're ugly."

"It wasn't because you wanted to learn to rope?" Parker dragged his hands through his brown hair. "I mean, we are just dumb cowboys who goof around with ropes and cows."

"No, you dumb man!" Charlotte shifted, grabbed hold of Parker's shirt, and pulled his face into her own. From the first time she watched The Cowboy Way videos, she had wanted to kiss him. She knew him. She had watched him for almost two years now. He was soft and kind under that tough, broody act. He never showed his feelings because, deep down, no one would believe a cowboy could be so sweet. She craved a quieter life. She wanted the escape from her own life.

This was what she needed. Someone to be tender to her, because she had been taught her whole life to be calloused and unfeeling. They brought her up to be the back-up monarch. Her sister would rule and she would never get the chance. In Charlotte's own mind, she was free to let her heart choose. And her heart wanted the brown-eyed cowboy in front of her.

Like a cobra striking the object in front of her, she devoured his plump lips. Her hands found the defined jawline of his face, keeping him where she wanted him. Unable to pull away, Parker's hands found their way to her low back, one of them sliding a little lower over the curves he had craved so much to look at. Her body sparked inside, wanting him to never release her. Quivering from how good she felt, filling his need to be with her, he pulled her body against his own. Holding her closer.

They stopped at the sound of an engine, fighting its way up the rocky pathway that led to the cliff side. Parker's cheeks blushed as he licked his swollen lips. His body screaming from inside of him to take her now. "That wasn't so bad, was it?" she asked, biting her bottom lip. Her blue eyes were almost black from the shadow of his hat.

"My hat suits you. You might want to get it cleaned, though." Parker rubbed the back of his neck. "Not sure it's worthy of a princess in that shape." He hesitated, placing a hand in his back pocket, only to pull it right back out.

Reaching up to pull the hat off her head, she brought it to her face and inhaled the inside brim. "I like it. It smells like leather and dirt. Like you."

Parker cringed. Little did she know how dirty that hat was. The sweat collection from his head could have filled up a five-gallon bucket. He had worn that hat every day for as long as he could remember and never washed it.

Charlotte put the hat back on her head. She brushed the side of his face. The scruff that he had let grow over the last two days felt like a mild sand paper. "Come on, cowboy, dreams don't last forever. I must go play princess now."

They walked hand in hand to where their horses were tied. Closer to the cars that had just pulled up. Mary bolted out of the back door, shoving the chauffeur, who wasn't fast enough to open her door, back a few steps. She stomped her boots, her arms swung from side to side as she pushed up the hill. "I can't believe…" she huffed. "That you had the audacity to leave like a spoiled brat." Mary scowled at Parker. "Just because I allowed them to come, doesn't mean you can do whatever you please. You have a duty to this country, young lady!"

Taking the reins of her big gelding from Parker, Charlotte rolled her eyes. "Mary, you'll never understand," she pulled herself up on the saddle, "I really don't want any part of your monarchy. For all I care you can go rule, and live happily ever after. I want nothing to do with it. I want to move away, far from here. Having no part of it." She turned the gelding around and nudged his sides toward home.

Mary stomped the ground and slapped her arms against her sides. "You ungrateful little—"

"Highness, shall we?" the chauffeur interrupted before she could finish the insult to her sister.

"Yes, thank you, Carson." Mary turned to glare at Parker. "I assume you know the way back?"

"I do, thank you."

Mary turned without even a smirk and paraded herself back to the car, where she waited for her door to be opened this time. Parker let out a sigh. He patted the red mare's neck. "I think I may be way in over my head." She seemed to understand as her big eye blinked a few quick strokes.

Parker rode back, enjoying the landscape of this foreign place. The air held a misty musk. The grasses were a deep dark shade of green, like moss in a river as it roared over the rocks underneath. The trees towered overhead, reaching for the clouds. The surroundings were full of happy foliage. This was strange to him, unlike Arizona in every way. The brownish red soil was full of dull sage bushes, cacti, and mesquite trees, which were a light yellowish green with sparse branches, thin leaves and thorns.

The wind sent a chill through his button down and he reminded himself to bring his jacket next time. When Parker finally reached the stable, he brushed down the mare and placed her back into her stall. He stuffed his hands into his pockets as a chill rolled over his skin, tiny bumps raised on his arms. His breath was visible as the sun settled behind the horizon. He hurried toward the little cottage he called home for the short time he was here and opened the front door.

"About time you showed," Chase said, his feet on propped up on the table again. At least this time, he had removed his boots. "What happened to your hat?" A cowboy's hat was a gem. It never left his head intentionally. If it happened to hit the ground, they retrieved it as soon it as possible. The hat was always hung, not placed.

Debating if he should tell his friend a fictional story or the truth of where his hat really was, he eyed him. He would eventually see where it had ended up if the princess continued to wear it. Parker sat down at the table where a plate of food sat covered and waiting for him. He dug in, still debating how he would tell Chase he had given his favorite hat to a princess who he could feel himself falling for. A princess who was so far out of his reach, he would have more chances of surviving a jump off a twenty-story building.

He placed his last bite of dinner in his mouth, grabbed his plate, rinsed it, and took in a deep breath. Hoping Chase would understand. "I let the princess keep it."

"You what?" Chase stiffened. Eyeing his friend with disbelief as he walked away. "Did I just hear you, right?" Chase was now talking to himself. "I can't believe this."

Parker turned in the hallway, ignoring him, and went into his room, brooding over a kiss he liked more than he knew he should. A kiss to a woman that was way out of his league.

Chapter 6 Birthday Rodeo

David arrived promptly an hour after sunrise. The three cowboys still sat at the table when he walked in, finishing an omelet and toast. "Good morning chaps." He pulled out a clipboard. "Today marks Princess Charlotte's birthday, and she has an entire list of festivities planned." He looked straight at Jason. "She does expect most of the day to be videoed and posted. Of course, keeping to the guidelines we agreed to in the contract."

"Of course," Jason nodded, feeling an urgent need to read over the contract again. Chase elbowed Parker.

"After you've finished breakfast, we are to all meet up in the large barn," David pointed, "that direction. I do hope that sheep are an applicable target for roping, as cattle were a tad difficult to come by on such short notice."

Parker folded his arms. One of his eyebrows rose as he eyed Chase. "This is going to be fun," Chase added.

"Yes, well, the princess wanted a rodeo of sorts for her birthday. We did our best to work with what we had."

"And what exactly does that all mean?" Chase questioned.

David let out an unsure laugh. "Most of our horses are not trained in—the acts of rodeo, so we have planned to do it on foot. I could obtain nothing that involved riding a wild bucking out-of-control animal." David shivered. "I still don't understand why anyone would want to risk their lives to ride something with such uncontrolled anger."

"The bronc horses are trained to buck. Most of them are sweet like puppy dogs. The bulls, well, they are just born rotten to the core." Chase pulled his hat from his knee and placed it on his head. "I'm sure we could get some of your warm-bloods to buck."

"No, the audacity!" David clutched the clipboard to his chest. "I'm sure that is, quite unnecessary."

"It might be more fun than roping sheep." Chase stood with his plate. "I hope we don't have to have to ride the poor creatures."

Parker laughed, also standing to return his plate to the sink. "Chase, I think mutton busting is no longer an option in your size."

"What?" Chase held his free hand to his heart. "You don't think the sheep could carry me?" Chase squatted down as if he were riding a sheep. He twirled his hand around in the air as he hopped around, imitating a bucking sheep. "Yeah doggie. Yeehaw. I'm the perfect size with a little squat."

David's face elongated as his eyes widened. "If I must say. That was quite disturbing."

"Chase, quit teasing the poor guy." Parker shook his head back and forth. "I promise, David, we aren't as uncivil as he makes us out to be. I'm sure whatever you have planned will work out just fine. We'll head over shortly."

"Thank you." David nodded toward Parker. "I will see you gentle-er, cowboys later, then." David left with a hustle through the front door.

Chase doubled over, holding his stomach with one hand, and slapping his knee with the other. "I can't believe this guy. He's so serious."

"He works for royalty. I don't think he is allowed to act any different."

"Yeah, but Park, did you see his face? I thought he was going to hurl, right here in front of us." Chase mocked David, and pretended to dry heave.

"He looked pretty appalled," Jason agreed. "I thought he was going to cancel the whole day and send us home."

"Nah, he doesn't have that kind of power. Besides, Parker here," Chase gave Parker's back one big loud slap, "has the princess wrapped around his little finger. Giving her his favorite hat and all."

"What was I supposed to do? Tell her to give it back?"

"Uh yeah, it's your hat." Chase mocked him, batting his eyes.

"I have a spare," Parker grumbled.

"Just don't get hurt. I don't want to watch you climb back out of that hole again."

"I know. I've already made a mental note to myself; there isn't any chance. I look at it this way. They paid for us to come here, have a vacation, and make some videos. The least I could do is give her a hat."

"Okay, I can't argue with that. Now go get your other hat, so we aren't late to rope some sheep." Chase waved Parker away, like he was a fly on the wall.

Parker had brought his hats together in a hat shipping container. This helped keep all the rims bent the way he liked them, undamaged. He pulled out his spare. It was brown; he had preferred the black one Charlotte had taken but this would do. He'd only worn it a few times, so this gave him a chance to get to know the new one. He eyed himself in the small mirror over the dresser, tipping his head to the side to see how the hat matched his face. The strong jawline, lined with his dark scruff, he looked good. Handsome. Satisfied, he left the room after grabbing his rope.

When the three cowboys entered the barn, their arms were full. Jason had insisted they bring all his equipment: three cameras, two stands, a foldable background canvas that Parker didn't think they would ever use, and a large light.

"Brilliant you made it," David said, clapping his hands together. "Let's set this up over here." He waved for them to follow. "This is perfect. We already had an area picked out for standalone photos. You can add your canvas and light where you think the pictures will turn out best."

There were two bales of straw stacked on one another and one on the side. Yellow, white, and pink daisies outlined a white archway. A pair of old worn-down cowboy boots, a metal sign that read: Farm Sweet Farm, and a stuffed rooster decorated the area. They added the canvas behind the hay and the light to the side. Jason set up one of his stands and cameras for still shots.

The barn, even though it was massive, smelled like sheep. Parker's nose crinkled. He didn't particularly care for the creatures. They rarely thought on their own. They only followed in a herd, bleating, and pooping all the time. A cow is a much larger target. He hoped his roping skill was still impressive.

Chase and Parker left Jason to his cameras, and they headed over toward the arena full of walking cotton balls, called sheep. Chase twirled his roped around to his side and back over his head, clearly showing off. As they approached, David introduced the princess.

Charlotte was wearing her tan riding jodhpurs, a tight riding jean, and a white button down, tucked neatly under a black belt. Her tall leather boots, the same ones Parker had helped pull off a few days before, covered her feet up to her knee. Her hair was pulled tightly into a bun like Parker had seen the first day he'd met her. She resembled a horseback riding ballerina.

"Where's your new hat?" Chase asked her.

"Hello to you too, Chase." Charlotte ran her hand over the slicked hair on the side of her head. "I didn't want to rouse my sister any further, so I left it safely on my bed."

Parker's eyes closed and his face wrinkled with a frown.

"Was that wrong?" she asked, noticing his face.

"That's like the number one, no, no rule with a cowboy hat. Never place it down. You should always hang it," Chase added.

"That's a silly rule. I assure you. The hat is perfectly safe."

"I'm sure it is. It's just that if there were a chance someone would forget and sat on it, the hat would be ruined."

The princess thought about this. Chase had made a good point and if the hat had meant anything to Parker, she could understand why his face had gone into an unpleasant cringe. She bit onto her lip. Thinking for a moment. Parker watched her, wishing he could nibble on her soft lips, making her giggle, as she begged him for more.

"David," Charlotte said, waving. "Could you have my maid run up to my room, find a proper place to hang my cowboy hat? It has come to my attention that it's not traditional to lay a hat on the bed as I have done."

David took a slight bow at his hips. "Yes, your highness. I'll send her a message at once."

"There," Charlotte said with a nod. "Now to my birthday festivities." The corner of her mouth rose slightly as she winked at Parker. His face burned as the heat filled it with red splotches. He ducked his head, allowing the brim of his hat to cover the evidence of the blush. "I want us to do a roping of sorts. I would have loved to do it on horses, but David said it was dangerous and that the sheep would most likely lose their little minds. They aren't the brightest of creatures."

Parker chuckled. "No, ma'am."

"They allowed me to order in a few ropes. I expect everyone to take part, even David."

"Highness, I. I will just, I would be better off supervising."

"No David, you will play along just like the rest of us."

"Very well then."

Chase elbowed Parker, then rubbed his hands together like a villain. "This is going to be good."

As a team effort, Carson, their driver, and David brought over a large box. It was big enough to place a body in. "Here are the props we will need. I won't make anyone wear anything they might feel uncomfortable with, but there are a few cowboy hats in here, too." Charlotte pulled out a stack of crisp new ropes. "Don't be shy, everyone. Grab one," she motioned to Chase and Parker, "except for you two, unless you don't want to use your own."

Like a brick wall, Carson stood next to the box he had placed, his hands locked behind him. Watching as David grabbed a rope and examined the foreign object. "Go on Carson, you too," Charlotte encouraged.

Carson bolted to one side, his hands stopping to his side, his eyes wide. "Excuse me, Highness, but I prefer to watch at a distance."

"No, kind sir, on my orders you will participate."

He nodded. Reaching in to the box to pull out a rope, his nose crinkled as he held it at a distance. Chase had already hopped the fence and took no shame in being the first to introduce the rope to the terrified sheep. He twirled and twisted, showing off his ease with the tool he had used since he was a small boy. Before he put it away, he widened the loop and jumped through it.

Hands on his hips, Parker watched. Unimpressed on how much attention Chase always insisted on. "Are you done yet?"

"Actually, if you all enjoyed it, I'll have another go."

"No, we are good." Parked shifted to the other foot, his spur whistled a little.

"It rather impressed me," David added shyly. He attempted to move his rope as Chase did. The rope crumpled out of his hand and landed in the soft arena dirt, in a messy pile. "Well, I guess it's harder than it looks."

"I'll go first," Chase said, bringing his rope up slowly so David could mimic, even though he was trying to figure out the knotted mess he had created. Chase swung two swings and lassoed one of the sheep in the front of the herd. It bleated, kicked out, and ran. Chase let go of his rope. "I let go so that he didn't hurt himself."

"Did you hurt the poor beast?" David asked.

Chase's lips thinned into a horizontal line. "Pfft, no. I just scared him a little."

"If I may be so kind," Carson set his rope down, "I must attend to my duties. It has been a pleasure, happiest of birthdays Princess."

"Oh, if you must Carson, but know I know you're using this as an excuse to get out of this." Charlotte pressed her lips into a thin line and blinked her eyes slowly. Bending at the hips as he held his hands behind him, Carson turned and left. "Don't even think about it, David," Charlotte said, just as he opened his mouth and then shut it.

Parker gave a brief lesson on how to swing and handle the rope. David caught on but would never throw the rope and look like he knew what he was doing. Chase retrieved the ropes. If the sheep were caught, Chase would run out and loosen the rope as they escaped.

"There you go," Parker said as he stood behind the princess. He only stood close enough to reach over and help guide her hand if she missed a twirl. His body felt like a volcanic mountain, this close to her. Sweaty and hot, he wanted more than anything to kiss her. She smelled of sweet lavender and clean soap. Alas, he could not, as they were being videoed.

Finally, in her last swing, she landed a perfect loop over the top of one of the sheep; it darted out from the herd, like a lightning bolt. Its feet striking the ground so fast, the princess had no time to think to let go.

Instead, in her moment she held tighter, her body plunged forward, landing with a loud thud on the ground. The terrified animal screamed as it dragged the princess. Dirt flew in her face and all her senses were numbed, except to the rope burn on her hands.

"Charlotte, let go!" they all shouted several times.

It wasn't until Parker ran up behind her and in the heat of the moment, not thinking of the consequences of slamming his body on top of the royal. He covered her body with his, careful not to squish her as he angled to the side. His large hands latched onto hers, prying her delicate fingers off the rope. Even in the excitement; his body betrayed him. He wanted her, craved her. She felt so right huddled next to him. He pulled in her tighter, cradling her as her body recovered. He told himself it was to help her and not to satisfy his lust. Her chest heaved. The powered dirt caked onto her face and added an outline to her dainty features. The bun that had been so perfectly placed on her head was undone, messy. Her coffee brown locks flowed over her shoulders and back.

When she opened her sapphire blue eyes to meet Parker's browns, he brought a finger up and traced her cheek; removing some of the dirt and taming a stray lock of hair. "You were supposed to let go." He couldn't help but smile at the woman he held in his arms. She was so beautiful, even caked in dirt.

"I didn't have time to think about that," she said, biting her lip. Without a care in the world, he allowed his desire for her to persist. He pressed his lips to hers. He laced his fingers into the back of her neck, tangling them in her hair as he tasted her. She followed him, and instead of pulling away as she should have, she moved herself closer, feeling his warmth.

A clearing of the throat was the only thing that finally stopped them. David towered over the two of them, staring down as he scratched his forehead. "If I may, your highness. I'm not sure how your sister will react to this." He waved his hand through the air. "We may need to delete this last part and not speak of it again. Jason?"

Jason nodded.

Parker stood up, giving a hand to Charlotte. Helping brush the remaining crumbles of dirt from her shirt, he avoided her lower backside. Though he wished he could run his hand over her curves, he resisted. "Yes, David, you're right. That was foolish." One of her blue sparkles snuck a glimpse at Parker. She didn't mean what she had said, but her status made her state otherwise.

When Parker's mind came back to reality, he realized Chase, Jason, and a few of the hired helpers that were working in the background had all come to a stop. They all stared, the whites of their eyes more evident than normal. "Jason, you'll be able to delete that last part?"

"Are you sure you want me to? I mean, the ladies are going to love it. It was like a little romance movie. The ladies love that stuff."

"Yes, it must be deleted, as stated in the contract about protecting the rights of the princess," David added matter-of-factly.

Chase leaned over to Jason's ear. "Just save it for our eyes only. Don't blast it on social. Yet." He winked.

"I think that will be all the cowboy fun for today. We need to have the princess checked over by a doctor to make sure she is unharmed," David said, bringing his clipboard to his chest.

"Really David, I'm fine," Charlotte insisted. "Just a little shook up."

"And the red liquid dripping down your arm, there?" David pointed, swirling around his index finger toward Charlotte's arm.

The princess lifted her arm to her eye's view. The skin had torn from the earlier event. Leaving a nasty open wound that would need cleaning. "Oh dear, I suppose I should get that looked at."

David ushered the princess toward the gate but stopped in front of the cowboys first. "We expect you for dinner in an hour in the palace. It's formal attire."

Chapter 7 Formal Dinner

A light knock on the cottage door startled Parker from a nap on the front room couch. With what only seemed like a moment, his groggy head told him his sleep had just begun. Jason, who was having a snack in the kitchen, answered to find Carson at the door. "Are you gentlemen ready?"

Jason stopped mid-air to place another grape in his mouth. He looked over at Parker, who was still on the couch. "Are we ready?" Jason repeated, his voice cracking.

It took Parker a few moments to get his mind to focus. He stumbled over the day's events until the small conversation he and David had had last in the arena. *Dinner at the palace*. "Crap!" He pulled at his brown hair. "Give us five minutes Carson," Parker held up his hand, spreading all his fingers out, "and we'll be right out."

Almost throwing himself off the sofa, he leaped to his feet. Parker rushed into Chase's room before stopping at his own. Chase was snoring, face down on his bed, boots still on his feet. His hat hung on a rack on the closet door. "Chase! My man, we are late for dinner at the palace." He jerked only a little, a small grumble came from his mouth and then he flipped his head around in the other direction. Parker grabbed hold of one of his shoulders and shook him gently. "Chase. Dinner. Palace. We are late!"

Like the scared sheep that scattered around that morning, Chase bound out of his bed. "What!" Parker watched Chase in his half-awake state, run out of the room and then return a few moments later, his hair standing in places and his face stamped from the bed quilt. He stopped part way through the doorway. "I don't even know why I ran out of the room."

Parker laughed. "It's okay man. I get it. Just get dressed as fast as you can. Something nice."

Finding his best button down, which wasn't much, Parker grabbed his hat from the hanger, slipped one boot on, and then hopped out the doorway with the other. The three of them met in the front room almost about the same time. All dressed in their best cowboy attire, with dirty boots and dusty hats.

The men left the cottage to find Carson waiting to open the passenger door of his car. One of his thick bushy eyebrows raised at the appearance of the cowboys. He said nothing of their offensive choice of clothing and kept his composure, gesturing for them to enter the car.

"Why do we need a car ride to the palace when we could walk?" Chase added as he lifted his rump to adjust his pants and belt.

"Maybe because we would have been even later than we already are?" Parker griped.

"The palace is over two miles from the cottage. We could have walked, but I prefer not to walk that far after dark in this cold," Jason said, pulling his jacket over his shoulders.

"I didn't realize it was that far." Chase rubbed his temples. "Man, I'm tired. How long did we sleep and what time is it?"

"It's five pm on the twelve-hour clock," Carson responded, looking in his rearview mirror. "I do remember David mentioning it was a formal dress?"

"Yes, Carson. I'm afraid this is all we have. It happens to be the nicest clothing we have with us." Parker fidgeted with the hat that sat on his lap. "I hope it's acceptable. If not, we can eat in the cottage. Ethel is an awesome cook."

"It didn't register in my mind that we might have to go into a castle with royal people. It won't be snobby curled up hair wigs and frilly collars, will it?" Chase questioned.

Clearing his throat, Carson tried not to laugh. "No, sir. They've done away with those." He rubbed his lips together, trying to find the best way to word his next sentence. "More of tie and dress pants or slacks would have been more appropriate. Jeans are very casual."

Throwing his head back and puffing out a sigh, Parker shook his head. "It is what it is."

The car pulled up in front of the palace drive. The enormous stone building was exactly what a castle looked like in any fairytale. Long corridors with slanted pitches met an occasional tower that pointed a cone shaped roof toward the clouds. Oblong windows dotted the openings to hallways and rooms. Stone carved pillars decorated the corners and midsections of the roofline. Greenery, perfectly etched and manicured, lined along some of the rocky walls. The damp humid air made a perfect combination for climbing vines and moss to make the walls their home.

All three of them stood staring at the massive structure, not sure it was real. Chase removed his hat to lean back far enough to see all the way to the highest tower. "I can't… I mean… Dang."

"I didn't think places like this actually existed," Jason whispered. "Or if they did, people didn't live in them anymore."

The thick oak wood door in front of them moaned loudly on its hinges, dwarfing the old man who opened it. "Good evening, gentlemen. Please step inside."

Turning back to thank Carson, Parker saw him nod as he bent down into the driver's seat of the car and then drove off. They followed the doorman through a large corridor of stone. Their footsteps echoed as the heel of their boots hit the rocky floors. Parker tried to keep his boot placement gentle, but it was no good. They would know the cowboys were coming.

As they approached the double doors at the end of their walk, the hallway veered to the left, but their guide stopped, pushed on the doors, and gestured for them to walk in.

Crystal chandeliers as big as cars hung every ten feet. The rock-like formations sent light prisms sparking throughout the room in all directions, almost blinding. A long table was set for twenty or more. Guests in intricate dresses and tailored suits filled the chairs. Cheeses, rolled meats, crackers, and garnish was decorated, and placed between flowered table settings with tall wine glasses, carved silverware, and matching plate sets, each one without a blemish in front of every seat. It was something the three of them had never expected to encounter in a lifetime. Back home, paper goods and red solo cups were just fine.

The chatter that pounded in their ear drums stopped instantly as the cowboys entered the room. All eyes, wide, staring at the men who just walked through the double doors. Their faces, blank, offended, maybe even alarmed. Chase cleared his throat as Parker dusted his collared shirt, smoothing it out. His rough fingers catching one button, luckily not ripping it off, he felt the back of his neck flash with heat.

Removing his hat, Parker held it to his chest. "Howdy," his voice quivered. Whispers flew across the tables like leaves in the breeze. Heads turned to the persons sitting next to one another. Clearly, they did not belong here.

Leaning into his friend, Chase lowered his hat to cover his face. "I'm thinking they don't approve of our get-up." The three cowboys fidgeted as they realized they hadn't taken the seriousness of this dinner.

The whispers of disapproval stopped, with the slow, sarcastic, rhythmical clap of Prince Alexander. The feet of his chair scratched the marble floors and pierced the ears of everyone inside the room. "Well done. That is one way to get all the attention on yourselves. Show up like dogs, full of dirt and…" He walked toward the three men, who had not moved since they had entered the room.

"And, well, I don't know what you call that." He used a finger to mimic them. "Are these your work clothes?" Alexander circled around them. Every eye in the dining hall glued to his every move. "Did you miss the memo that this was a formal event?"

Placing his hat back on his head, Chase puffed out his chest with a humble grin. "Thanks for noticing. The nice thing about our clothes here is we can use them for both work and formal attire."

Prince Alexander burst out in laughter; the rest of the room followed him. When he finally stopped, he held his hand to his mouth, acting as if another laugh might escape if he didn't hold it in. "I see." He walked around to his side of the table, but before he ventured back to his seat, he stopped. "I'm afraid in this palace, this room is for people who know how to dress appropriately. Please see yourselves out the door you came in."

Taking a step forward, and stopping, Chase felt his blood boil to the surface of his skin. "Excuse me?" His fists formed into tight balls and veins bulged from the tops of his hands. "We were invited to dinner tonight."

The prince only laughed, never bothering to turn around, furthering his lack of acknowledgement. Parker reached out to Chase's arm, grabbing his enlarged bicep. "Not here, my brother," he whispered.

Chase ripped his arm from Parker's grip, his anger from being insulted fueling a fiery dragon inside of him. He ripped his hat off his head and slammed it into Parker's chest for him to hold. Safe with his brother from another mother. Knowing he couldn't stop his friend now, Parker held onto his friend's prized possession.

Stomping his feet in a brisk walk, he turned the prince around. "How dare you tou—ch." But before the prince could finish his sentence, Chase landed his fist on Alexander's right cheek. His head snapped to the side with the impact. Spit soared through the air, landing on a woman sitting at the table. She screamed out in disgust, wiping the slime from her forehead immediately. Alexander grabbed his face, lifting his hands to find a missing tooth covered in red spit. He cried out like a little boy who had dropped his lolly in the dirt.

Chairs scuffled, and the guests ran in all directions as Mary stood yelling for the guards. "Contain these fools," she growled, pointing at the three cowboys.

"I guess that means dinner is off?" Jason asked, still standing next to Parker.

"I'm thinking so. Leave it to Chase to start a brawl."

A couple of palace guards pulled their arms behind them, binding their hands. "Come on lads, to the holding chamber." Parker and Jason didn't fight. Chase let his pride get in the way.

"You think you can tie me?" He backed up from the two guards in front of him, raising his fists. "There is no way you're taking me alive."

"Now, sir, let's be reasonable. No one is in trouble. We just want a quiet place to talk," the guard tried to reason.

Glancing over his shoulder before the guard guided him out of the room, Parker said, "Chase, just let them do their thing. Come on, man, it's not worth it."

Heat bubbled inside of him. Chase was ready to fight. His triggers were set, and he needed to fight to get closure. He growled, breathed out and let a pinch of common sense back into his mind, as he watched the other guards escort his friends out of the dining hall.

"Fine, I'll go, but you won't bind my hands," Chase said, pointing a finger at the guard. "No way in hell. He insulted me first. I had every right to punch the jerk."

The guard opened his mouth to say something, then decided not to. Instead, he nodded and gestured for Chase to follow his friends.

***

They left the three American friends, hands unbound, in a large room. One desk sat regally in the back; it faced the chairs they sat in. "Chase, did you really have to punch him?"

"Listen Park, the guy is a douche-bag, and yeah, I did."

"We could have just reasoned with the d-bag," Jason suggested.

"You two are insulting the cowboy way. We don't back down to pansies. We fight, stand up for our pride."

"But he's a prince who's going to be their king one day." Parker's hands rubbed his forehead under the brim of his hat.

When the door behind them opened and Mary stomped her way in, the three of them went silent. Would she press charges? She wasn't the type to let things go without punishment. Would she sentence them to spend the rest of their lives in prison, never able to return home? Mary said nothing. She turned around the corner of the desk, dragging her finger along the edge before she faced them and sat in the chair that resembled a throne.

A loud breath escaped her mouth, before she brought her hands in front of her face and laced her fingers together, all but two. Her index pointer pressed up against her lips as her scowl looked over each of them. The silence, deafening. Parker used the brim of his hat to hide his eyes. Chase folded his arms over his chest, ready to fight back the second she threw insults.

After dragging her finger off her lips and over one side of her cheek, Mary placed her hands in front of her on the desk. "I've yet to deal with something like this. I'm actually not that upset." She smiled. "Alex deserved that punch. It wasn't your fault. We didn't ask if you needed formal attire. I should have known to ask. I'm sorry about that. I will not apologize for his behavior, but I can't let punching our future king in front of our guests go unpunished."

A wave of relief washed over the three of them. It surprised them that Mary wasn't mad, and even more that she apologized. Mary, the one they thought disliked them, had almost sided with them.

"Any ideas? I'm open to them." She untangled her hands and opened the drawer on the side of her desk to bring out a pad of paper and a pen. "I had thought maybe to send you home. Or maybe even some sort of public humiliation. But that was in the past. We are more civil now."

Jason raised his hand like a little boy in grade school. "Maybe we could publicly apologize to Alexander?"

Mary shook her head. "No, Alex doesn't deserve that. He was out of line. A complete abuse of his power, he will be reprimanded. I will not tolerate actions of that manner in my kingdom. I could've stopped him, and I'm sorry. It just didn't seem right to scold him in front of our guests."

Nodding, they agreed. Mary was more of the leader than she let them believe. It was important to her that her kingdom was running the right way. She had come across as a pompous princess who'd inherited riches and power. Alone with her in the room, they could all see that her kingdom mattered to her.

"After going over the situation in my head, I would have wanted to punch him, too. I often still do. They arranged our marriage, uniting our two kingdoms. You all know the drill. He's a tad arrogant and immature and he's used to getting his way."

"A tad?" Chase questioned, as his left eyebrow raised.

"Your temper exceeds his, Mr. Chase."

"Well, I..." Chase reached back and scratched an invisible itch on his neck. "I sometimes get excited and go right to swinging my fists."

"So then, mucking stalls for the day tomorrow? Sound fair enough?"

"Sure, the three of us can manage that fine enough."

"No. Only you. If I remember right..." Mary nodded to where Jason and Parker sat quietly. "Your friends here didn't throw any fists."

Pressing his lips together firmly, Chase nodded. "Very well then."

"Good, then it's settled. As for you two. We will have a picnic outside, at mid-day. You're invited and you can wear your cowboy attire. You can bring Chase a plate once you're finished. We don't want him to go hungry."

"Thank you, Mary," Parker said, pulling his hat off to his chest.

"Of course. Try to stay out of trouble this time." Mary closed her eyes and rubbed at her temples. "And if you must have relations with my ill-behaved sister, do it where no one can see you. The servants' gossip. At least try to keep it clean. My sister's reputation is everything."

Chase threw an elbow into Parker's rib. He grunted. "Yes, ma'am. I understand."

The three of them stood and left for their little cottage where Ethel had been instructed to cook them a dinner in place of the one they had missed. In a place they wouldn't cause anymore drama for the evening.

CHAPTER 8 A ROYAL APOLOGY

The smells of breakfast woke the three cowboys up early. Freshly grilled potatoes, eggs and sausage wafted in the air. Chase had eaten and was out the door by the time Parker had joined Jason at the table. "What's the plans today, my friend?"

Smiling, Jason finished chewing. "They want me to film Chase shoveling manure in the royal stables so everyone can know he served out his sentence." He took a drink of juice. "At some point, he is to meet with Alexander. They don't have to apologize, but Mary wants them to shake hands for the camera."

"That seems fair enough to me," Parker added, as he stabbed a sausage link with his fork. The savory spices melted in his mouth as he chewed. "Ethel, as always, this is divine."

"Thank you, Parker. I'm glad you like them," Ethel said, wiping her hands on her apron. "This is for you." She slid a small piece of paper next to Parker's plate. She patted his shoulder and walked off.

Unfolding the paper, Parker glanced over its message. It was short and simple: Meet me; you know where. Charlotte.

"What is that all about?" Jason inquired, finished his last bite of eggs. Sitting close enough, he had glanced over to read the suspicious note.

"Nothing."

"Ah ha! Meeting in secret with the princess again." Jason aimed his imaginary hand guns at Parker.

"What? No!"

Jason gave Parker a scowl, his eyes narrowed. "C'mon, I know you better than that."

"Fine, yes." Parker shook his head, rubbing his forehead. "Can I really refuse a princess?"

Jason laughed. "No, you can't." He stood, walked behind Parker, and placed his hands on his shoulders. He massaged the tight muscles. "Relax my man. It will be fine. She's not another Briel."

At the sound of her name, Parker's heart clenched. The pain hitting his memories like a slap to the face. Her soft skin, her sky-blue eyes sparking against the freckles that dotted faintly against her pale skin. The brunette curls of her hair tickling his face when he held her. He could almost smell the strawberry and crème, shampoo with the thought.

When Parker realized Briel had dumped him, his world crashed. She'd left him standing alone at the altar, his eyes closed and his shoulders slumped, the feelings of abandonment wanting to crush him all over again. Jason stopped, knowing Parker was letting the hurt surface. "Hey, don't let her get to you. Move on, take this princess crush, and run with it. Let her help you forget. Even if it's only for a short time."

"You're right," Parker agreed. "I need to move on."

"Yes, you do." Jason gently punched Parker's shoulder. "I'll show you the video footage later on today. I'm sure Chase will cause some sort of drama." He rolled his eyes. "Go have fun. And let your heart open a little, just so it can learn to let go."

"Thanks man."

"And remember, you don't have to commit. We are on vacation, just let things play out. Enjoy the rare chance you get to have a fling with a princess. Lucky dog."

Nodding his head, Parker knew Jason was right. He didn't have to fall in love with the princess or worry that she would leave him the day before they were supposed to get married. Mary had made it very clear there was no chance of that. He would just try to have fun, let their mutual attraction for one another clear his head. Help him heal his heart and allow it to let love in again.

After Jason left, Parker helped Ethel clean up the kitchen, and she left for the day. He grabbed a glass of cold water and sat on the couch to pull his boots on. He rubbed the worry out of his face and took one last inhale before he headed to the stables to find a horse already saddled and waiting.

"Good morning, sir," the young stable hand's voice quivered. "Princess Charlotte asked me to wait here with a saddled horse. She said you would know where to find her."

Tipping his hat, Parker took the reins of the familiar red mare. "I do. Thank you?"

"Oh right, Gavin. My name is Gavin." The boy gestured to himself, bowing slightly.

"Thanks Gavin. I appreciate you saddling her up. Would you be offended if I gave back this silly hunk of leather and just rode the mare bareback?" Parker gave a silly grin. "I think I'd feel more comfortable without it."

"No, sir, please. I'm here to help you feel as comfortable as possible."

"Good." Parker lifted the large flap of leather to reveal two buckles. He loosened them and pulled the saddle that weighed almost nothing, and handed it to the groom. "Thank you."

"Have a lovely ride."

Again, he tipped his hat. "Will do." Parker grabbed a chunk of the mare's red mane, stepped behind her shoulder, and lunged himself forward, landing on her back in one solid motion. He glanced over just in time to see Gavin's eyes grow large. Unable to contain his pride, one side of Parker's mouth lifted. He nudged the mare forward softly with the heels of his boots and she trotted out of the barn, heading toward the ruins.

It felt good to ride. The cool wind threatened to bring tears to his eyes. The muscles of the horse underneath of him powered in a melodic rhythm as she loped across the grassy hillside.

Parker saw the slender silhouette of the princess from far. She wore his black cowboy hat, a blue blouse and a pair of jodhpurs that shaped her backside nicely. She was swinging the rope she had kept secretly stowed in the hole of the crumbling walls. When she swung the rope, her hips followed in a back-and-forth motion. He bit down on the side of his lip to contain his laughter.

Placing her hands on her slender hips, as he neared, Charlotte narrowed her eyes. "What is so funny, cowboy?"

"It's not every day I see a princess with a rope." He kept the part about how he enjoyed watching her butt swing around and blamed it on her attire. Most equestrians who wore that kind of get up in America wouldn't be caught dead with a rope and a cowboy hat.

"There is something else, isn't there?" She quickly snapped her head back, doing her best to examine her backside. Rubbing up and down her curves with her hands. Parker rolled his head, popping a kink in his neck, feeling a little jealous of her hands.

"Tell me," she demanded.

"Do I sense a weakness in the confident princess?"

"No!" Charlotte stiffened her posture. "I just noticed you staring… And laughing."

"I don't recall laughing."

"Well… You… You were grinning."

Tipping a head to the side, he ran his tongue over his teeth, deciding how he would explain his attraction to a beautiful woman rocking her hips back and forth in very form fitting clothing. "Can't a guy appreciate the pleasant view in front of him?"

"I—I suppose I can't keep you from thinking." She stomped her right boot, assuring she had a strong footing below her. "I guess…" Charlotte's face turned red, the heat of embarrassment flooding her mind. Spots sent her vision to near nothing, and it took her a moment to continue to stand upright.

Swinging his right leg over the red mare, Parker thumped the ground as he landed next to this horse. He led her over to Charlotte's large gelding and tied her up. He patted her neck once, giving her permission to graze on the tall damp grasses below them.

"Your rope swing is looking better." Parker grabbed a stick off from a nearby tree, yanking off it off the branch and placed it in to his mouth. It served no purpose other than, he felt, it might boost his confidence ever so slightly. He envisioned how cool the guys in the movies looked when they did it. "How are the sores healing up from the other day?"

Lifting her arms, Parker winced. Freshly scabbed over wounds lined her arms from her wrists to her elbows. "They might leave a mark," she joked.

"Nah, they'll heal up if you keep the right salve on them." Parker pointed a finger at her. "And don't you go picking at them." He gently fingered the side of the skin that wasn't torn up. "Yeah, it got you good. Just think what a cow might do if a silly sheep did this."

The princess watched the cowboy as he closely examined her arms. She liked his touch. His hands were calloused from working long hours outside, yet they were still warm. Her body trembled with the need to hold him as she eyed the strong jawline clenched over the stick he held in his mouth. His brown eyes reminded her of chocolate, soft and tempting. Something she always craved. Needed.

"Looks like the dirt won," he teased. Parker's eyes lifted from the scabs on her arms to find her blues watching him. A lightness in his chest and a fluttering in his belly brought a quick smile to his lips. Charlotte's face flushed. She pulled her arms down in a flash, the rope flopping to the ground.

Stumbling to pick it up, she stopped to find his hand on top of hers. The heat of the closeness of his body sent shock waves down her arms and into her chest. Heaving up and down, her pounding heart took over. Without thinking, and unable to control herself, she reached out and pulled the stick from the handsome cowboy's mouth and took his lips onto her own with one yank of his shirt.

The kiss was one of raw motion. There was no pattern, or leader. It was pure attraction. The drive of man meets woman. A pull of desire, the excitement of the new. Wanting of the forbidden. For Parker, it was the first step into the mending of the hole in his heart. The lightness in his soul rejoiced as he opened to the idea of love, even if he knew it wouldn't last.

Wrapping his arms around her slender waist, he pulled her against him. No longer jealous of watching her trace her curves. He took what he wanted, fueling his need that only increased into more. A lust. Greedily never satisfied until he took it all. Until he could claim her for himself.

Charlotte's fingers dug into his chest, bringing him to a stop in his carnal thoughts. He cupped her delicate face, tracing his thumb over her swollen lips. "We should be careful."

Inching closer, begging for more, she stood on the tips of her toes to reach his lips. "Why? I know what I want. I've known since the first time I saw you riding a horse. The dirt swarming you and the beast as you swung the rope over your head to lasso the horned creature."

Closing his eyes, Parker took a long exhale into the heavens. "We are from two separate worlds. In a few days, I'll go home. Return to trying to save my dad's ranch and keep it in the family. And you will stay here, as the political figure you're born to be."

"No," she said, pushing on his brawny chest. "They don't need me. I can come with you. Work the ranch with you." Her eyes pleaded.

Parker massaged the sides of his jaw with one hand. The brim of his hat covered his face as he looked down at his shuffling boot. "I want that, but I'm broken. I've been broken for some time. Broken attracts broken. Not that I am saying you're broken, it just wouldn't be fair to you. Until I can heal, it just wouldn't be right."

"Parker," her voice softened. Charlotte gently caressed his face. "Let me help you. Tell me what happened."

Turning to walk away, he took a few steps and returned. He stuck his hands into his jean pockets, causing his muscles to bulge from the white t-shirt he wore. "I'm not sure you want to hear it. That makes me weak to bring up the past." Parker shook his head. "It's not important anyhow."

Approaching him, she took a hand from one pocket. She laced her fingers through his. "Tell me. I want to know."

Again, he covered his face with his free hand to hide his emotion as he looked down at the ground. Silence stood between them. The chirping of birds in the nearby trees seemed to magnify. The rustling of the soft breeze in the leaves was vibrant, almost singing. Grinding of the horse's teeth behind him almost echoed in his mind.

"Parker, it doesn't make you weak to talk about it. It strengthens you. It helps to let it out." The princess squeezed the cowboy's hand.

Rocking back a little on his heels, his proud frame showed vulnerability. He rubbed under the brim of his hat, looking away, anywhere but at the beautiful woman in front of him. He took his hand from hers and sighed.

"There was this girl. We grew up in the same town. We went to school with one another, had classes together, that whole thing." Parker waved his hand. "Everyone knew we would get hitched one day. We did everything together. All our firsts shared." He chuckled, replaying a memory in his head. "The hay got everywhere."

Parker walked around his circle again. She watched him let off the hurt. He rubbed his eyes, drying them. She waited, allowing him to tell his story in his own time.

"She got pregnant." He ran his tongue over his teeth to conceal the tears that welled in his eyes. "Her parents weren't happy. Matter of fact, they hated me for it. Her dad came the night he found out. Fuming. Threats flew around the room like swarming bees. I promised him I would marry her. Take care of her and the baby." His voice trembled. Revealing the past he'd fought so hard to conceal.

Charlotte reached out and rubbed the side of his arm. "Oh, Parker. You did the right thing."

"We planned the wedding. Her belly grew, and we named the baby…" Parker paused. A small tear trickled down his cheek. Charlotte held her hand to mouth, knowing something had happened to the baby.

"Garth… After our favorite county singer." Parker paced another circle. "She called one night, crying. Her sobs were so much I couldn't understand a word she was saying. So, I jumped into the truck and headed over to her house. Ready for what her daddy would say or do. I didn't care because I loved her. I would have done anything she asked." Parker took a deep breath. "Her dad told me he had called a lawyer. They set up the adoption papers without me. Taking away all my rights, because we hadn't been married yet."

"That's horrible," Charlotte added.

"Briel and I had still planned to get married regardless of her parents, but the day before, she wouldn't answer my phone calls. I drove back over there and there was a letter taped to the door. They addressed it to me. Telling me she had left to go stay with her aunt in California. She didn't love me anymore and our son would be adopted to a nice family where he would grow up never knowing who I was."

Parker took off his hat and ran his fingers through his hair. "I was an idiot. I didn't cancel the wedding. I hoped that love would conquer all. She would come running down the aisle and we would run away together. Instead, I was wrong. I stood there, by that altar alone, waiting like a love sick imbecile. Our guests' whispers still echo in my mind. Humiliated by the woman I loved, broken, I crumbled that day."

Charlotte wrapped her arms around Parkers, trapping him in a tender embrace. "I'm so sorry, Parker. No one should have to go through that. But for whatever reason, you did. It has made you a better person." She released him and stuck a finger into his hard muscle abs. "It made you who you are today and brought you to me."

Chuckling, Parker put his hat back on his head. "I guess it did." He knew it could never be. The two of them were too different. He rubbed his lips together and took it for what it was. The first step to healing. "Pick up that rope. We got some tree stumps to lasso."

CHAPTER 9 CARRIAGE RIDES AND TEAHOUSES

Parker woke the next morning to the singing of Chase. His ears practically rang with the awful tones his friend belted out.

"I've got friends in low places," Chase bellowed. "Where the whiskey drowns and the beer..."

"Chase, my friend," Parker said, coming around the corner only dressed in his underpants. "If you need some tunes, we can pull some up on my phone. But please spare my ears."

"What you don't like my singing?"

Walking over to the kitchen, he pulled the peel off a banana, his eyes never leaving his friends. "Are you serious?" Parker took a bite and chewed, still staring at Chase. "You could have killed someone."

"I'm so ready to go home. I miss the dirt on my face. This place is too green, and their saddles are making me chafe."

Parker laughed and took a seat next to his friend on the couch. "I've been riding bareback."

"Why didn't I think of that?"

"Because you are Chase..."

Chase punched Parker's shoulder. "What is that supposed to mean?"

"Hey, ouch," Parker moaned, through a mouth full of banana. "Nothing. I love you, man. You just suck at singing."

"So, you and the princess?" Chase's left eyebrow lifted a few times, his face formed into a salty grin.

"No," Parker frowned, "nothing like that. A few kisses maybe."

"Well, you were out most of the night. What the heck did you do?"

"We talked a little. Roped on and off the horses. She is getting pretty good, actually."

"And?"

"That was it. I can't start something with someone that can't ever be."

"It doesn't have to be anything. You just take a little and then go home."

Parker nodded. "You're horrible."

"And that, my friend, is why I get laid and you don't." Chase stood up. "I'm off to shower." He stretched out his arms to the ceiling, a large yawn followed. "Last day, my man. I can't wait to get home."

Watching Chase walk away, Parker sighed. He fiddled with his banana peel as he thought how different things could have gone if he were more careless, like Chase was. The guy was a rock star. He never let the little things get to him. If he was down, it was never for long. He smiled, moved on and was onto the next challenge. And he was right, he always got the girl. Never once could Parker remember a time Chase didn't claim a girl he was after.

With Charlotte, though, it was different. He couldn't bring himself to feel that hurt, that aching in his chest again. He shook his head, disappointed in himself that he couldn't be more like Chase, and live freely. Instead, he was broody; he got attached and he let himself get hurt.

The sulking quickly diminished when no other than the princess herself barged unannounced through the front door of the cottage. She didn't have his hat on. Instead, a purple lady's hat matching the dress she wore. The brim extended out further on one side than the other. She took it off and placed it on the hanger next to the door.

A circlet of brown braids wound around her head in a shape of a crown. The dress that covered her small frame fitted around her feminine curves in the bodice. The rest of the purple material flowered down with lace showing at the bottom of the frilly skirt around her ankles.

Parker sat there on the couch, admiring her. She scuffed her feet with whatever her boots had picked up outside on the mat, and pulled the gloves off her hands. It wasn't until then that she looked around the quaint cottage to see him watching her. Her cheeks reddened not because she had realized he was watching her, but because he was practically naked.

That bronze skin of his rippled six pack, free from a shirt. Freedom ran over his defined muscles. Everything showing except for what was under his boxer briefs. His coffee-colored hair was still messy from sleep. She stood frozen, her heart pounding, her will to say something, anything disappeared from her mind. Only able to stare at the man she had lusted over all these months, sitting in front of her, vulnerable yet confident. Did he not care? Was he not ashamed he was just there, as he was?

"Good morning, Charlotte. Was there something I could help you with?"

"I. You. Naked. Blast! You should get dressed." Charlotte turned away, unable to keep her head straight. Hoping to hide her embarrassment.

Parker didn't move, except to pull his hands to his sides, rubbing over the bumpy muscles. Possibly suggesting his innocence. He glanced down at himself, shrugging. "Everything of importance is covered."

Charlotte returned to look at him. Her hand quickly rubbing her flushed cheek, then her neck, relieving a sweaty itching feeling that was surfacing. "Well, I—I thought I could take you into town." Her voice quivered, and silently she cursed herself for the lack of control. Her eyes would not obey. She couldn't help but to let them wander over the man on the couch. "Mary is allowing it with an escort. I thought Jason could video you and Chase experiencing a new—" she huffed out, fanning her warm face, "an unfamiliar experience."

Pausing mid-sentence, her eyes widened. Chase rounded the corner, rubbing a towel on his freshly showered blond hair. His bronzed skin and muscles bulged as he tightened them. Only a small towel was hinged at his waist. It looked as if at any moment it could fall to the ground and scar her innocent eyes forever.

"I think that'd be great," Chase added.

Parker chuckled. He knew the princess was uncomfortable. Part of him enjoyed it. He brought his hand to his mouth to keep from exploding into a deeper laugh.

The princess's chest rose and fell heavily as she concealed her emotions. She forced her eyes to the ground. She blew air through her lips, keeping the explosion that was happening inside of her from escaping. "Great. Then. I'll see you shortly." She turned, waving her hand behind her. "Make sure your clothing is — more appropriate."

Before she made it out the door, Parker stood. She kept her back to him as she quickly placed her gloves back on her hands. "What, my birthday suit isn't suitable? It could be fun to go out with just my boots and my hat. Might get me some Chase fame."

Charlotte turned to see him standing in his underwear. Red patches of embarrassment flooded her face and neck. She opened her mouth to say something and nothing came out. She grabbed her hat and practically burst out the door.

"I think you scarred her for life, Park," Chase said, still in his towel. He walked down the hallway to Jason's room and threw the wet towel he had used for his hair at the large lump under the blanket on the bed. "Wake up, sleepyhead. We are going to do some vlogging in town."

Twenty minutes later, the three cowboys had walked out the front door of their cottage to find two horse-drawn carriages parked in the driveway.

"What is this?" Chase questioned, his face beaming. "Jason, get those cameras out. This is going to be classic."

Of the two carriages, one was a large passenger coach, which Charlotte invited both Chase and Parker into. The second one was a Meadowbrook, an open type carriage big enough for the driver and one passenger. This is where they had Jason sit, so that he could video, openly.

They drove the horses down the gravel road that led to a paved one all the way into town. "So, is this carriage riding something you do often?" Chase asked.

Charlotte shrugged. "It used to be the only way we traveled before cars."

"How old are you?" Chase's right eyebrow rose.

"Chase," Parker elbowed his friend, "you never ask a lady her age."

Chase blew out a puff. "She said *we*, like she had lived a really long time." He threw up his hands, waving off the stupid remark. "I don't know she could be fae or something."

"Fae? What the heck is that?"

"You know, like fairies and elves, and vampires, they've got like magic and stuff, so they live like a long time."

Adjusting the skirt of her dress, Charlotte cleared her throat. "If you two are done talking about non-sense, then I could tell you I meant my family before me." She rolled her eyes. "I'm still quite young. From time to time, I enjoy a carriage ride. I thought maybe you could also appreciate such an opportunity."

"No, this is great, you're right, it's a rare thing to ride to town in a coach," Parker added, to ease the conversation. He sent a smug smirk in Chase's direction.

Chase held up his hands to his sides in an innocent motion and mouthed, "What?"

When the coach came to a stop, Jason was ready and waiting. Parker placed his hat on and stepped out of the coach steps after Chase. Making his grand exit, Chase lifted his arms to the sky. "Well folks, this is how travel was back in the day. Of course, us cowboys only used this sort of vehicle on long trips."

Parker rolled his eyes as he gave Charlotte his hand to help her down the steps. Their eyes met as she neared the ground. Heat boiled inside of him, and he watched her blush and glance away.

"This way, we are headed to the teahouse for lunch." Charlotte waved for them to follow.

"The teahouse?" Chase grimaced at Jason.

No wonder Charlotte had dressed in her fancy Victorian dress and hat. If the teahouse was anything like what the movies portrayed. He could only imagine how well this was going to go. Not well at all. Was she trying to set them up for an unpleasant experience before they left? He only hoped whatever happened, Jason got it all on video.

They walked up to a small white house. Its roof was covered in hay, and bricks lay on this exterior. Cobblestones lined the pathway to the front door. Bushes shaped into animals surrounded them. Flowers of all colors covered the area: blues, pinks, yellows, whites, not one patch of ground left uncovered. If fairies were real, this would have been the place they would have lived.

"Should we have dressed up?" Chase asked, his voice sounded a little worried. "I feel like our cowboy attire might not fit well here."

She tossed her head, looked back over her shoulders, peering out under the large brim of her purple hat. Charlotte smiled. "No. You're with me. No one will bat an eye."

"I have a feeling this will not go well," Chase leaned over and whispered to Parker.

"Just say nothing too stupid, ok?"

"Me?" Chase shrugged the comment off his shoulder, his fingers flicking away imaginary dust. "Never." He winked.

"Yeah, you."

Of course, as they entered, every head turned. Every highly decorated woman in a fancy hat. They were the only three men in this entire establishment. Parker felt his insides turn eight different directions. Sweat beads formed at the brim of his hat and he hoped they didn't run down his face as fast as he wanted to return through the door he just entered.

They followed Charlotte through the main dining hall. Whispers covered by gloved hands flowed like a stream. Every table now gossiped about the two unruly cowboys who followed the princess into a teahouse. Jason followed behind them, catching every detail on camera. Just as Parker thought they would survive, Chase had to put in his two-cents.

"Nothing to see here, ladies," Chase stopped, posing. Puffing out his chest slightly. He looped one of his thumbs on his buckle. "Yup, won this myself, riding a bull."

Gasps were heard all around the room. Whispers like a windy breeze traveled through the room.

"Don't worry, I knew how to handle the massive animal as it thrashed around trying to end my life."

Parker sighed and aggressively rubbed his forehead under his hat.

"Eight seconds." Chase moved around the room, weaving through the tables of ladies. Every eye glued to him. "Which seems like a lifetime. The pure, raw thrill of the ride. The adrenaline pumping through my veins, my heart threatening to pound out of my chest…" He made his way to a pretty woman his age and dropped to his knees, grabbing her gloved hand in his own. Her face reddening as the blush of attraction overcame her. "And then the buzzer clears all sense of doubt."

Chase kissed the white glove, and the lady brought the other to her mouth. "All so I could be here to woo this beautiful woman in front of me." Chase pulled his hat off and held it at his heart.

"Oh, sir," she said, her own chest now heaving in and out, "you are too kind." She waved her free hand in front of her flushed face.

"If I could, but kiss thy lips, it would give me the strength to continue," Chase said.

Shaking his head, Parker quickly made it to Chase's side and pulled his friend to his feet. "Not today, cowboy." He tipped his hat. "Sorry ma'am."

The pretty ladies' face was still red from the handsome cowboy encounter. She watched them as they left the room. All the surrounding women were green with envy, touching her shoulder and asking if she was all right. Acting as if the dirty, gorgeous man who had left them all swooning had molested her.

Already seated, Charlotte laughed as the two cowboys entered the private room. "Did you need me to have her brought to your cottage later, Chase?" She buttered a biscuit. "That was dear Anne, the Duke's daughter. She was quite taken by you. I believe she is still recovering."

They both sat down. Parker poured himself a glass of water, wishing it was whiskey. Jason quickly packed his camera into a safe place and joined them. "This is going to give us so much great feed."

"Does Chase always have to be the center of attention?" Charlotte asked.

"Most of the time," Parker answered.

"Do not," he defended himself. "Well, maybe. I mean, look at me. Can you blame them?" He held both hands out to his sides.

"Shame, I think Parker should get some attention sometimes, too. Or even Jason," Charlotte added as Parker blushed at her comment.

"Hey, it's just who I am. Parker is the strong, silent one. I keep the ladies at bay while Jason helps keep the background entertainment moving."

"Interesting. I guess you all play your part." Charlotte took a sip of her tea. "I have a going away gift for the three of you."

A server came through the door holding three large boxes. He set a wrapped box in front of each of the cowboys. They sat there stunned, unable to decide what to do. "Go ahead, and open them," Charlotte insisted.

The sounds of rustling and ripping paper echoed through the room to reveal three hat boxes. Inside was a custom-made cowboy hat for each of them. Parker pulled out his first. It was a deep chocolate brown, almost as dark as the one she had taken. On the underside of the brim, they embroidered his name and on the other side was Blossom. Chase and Jason also had similar stitching with their name and horse's name.

"This is incredible, Charlotte. Thank you," Parker said, still admiring his new prize.

"Yes, thank you," both Jason and Chase said.

"It was hard to find a shopkeeper who made the American style here. But I had him recreate the ones I saw you wearing on your shows. Jason's horse was the hardest to get the name for, as he is the least talked about."

"I'm lost for words. This is the best thing anyone has ever done for me," Parker confessed, his voice trembled slightly. He placed his current hat in the box and replaced the new on his head.

Biting her lip, Charlotte admired her gift for the handsome cowboy. The dark brown felt she had chosen pulled out the golden hints in the brown of his eyes. It highlighted the daily growth of the scruff that outlined his masculine jawline. She fidgeted in her seat, almost unable to control the urge to pull him to her lips. "It looks good on you, cowboy."

He tipped his new hat. The curves in his smile brought a wave of heated butterflies to her abdomen. The moment was quickly over when the server arrived with a plate of sandwiches and tarts.

"More tea will be out shortly," the server added. "Followed by a warm cheesecake topped with strawberries."

"My mouth is watering from the sound of it," Jason said, grabbing a sandwich in each hand.

Chase was still admiring the stitching on the brim of his new hat. "I just don't understand how he got that to look so perfect." He traced the letters with his fingers.

"It's not rocket science, my friend." Parker patted his shoulder. "They have fancy machines that do it nowadays."

"Wow," Chase said, scratching his blond head in awe. "Thank you. Really, this is exceptional."

"You're welcome. I know your trip wasn't the smoothest of vacations, but I do hope you enjoyed it. And I'm looking forward to seeing the videos Jason posts."

"Oh, this trip's videos are going to be epic," Jason said, after swallowing a bite of his lunch. "And thank you. I also love my hat."

"My pleasure. I hope that one day I can come visit you guys at the ranch."

"Make sure you bring clothes that can get dirty. It's basically the opposite of this place," Jason teased.

They finished their lunch and this time Charlotte showed the men out the back door so that they didn't draw so much attention to the ladies in the main room. The carriages took them home and ended with an uneventful trip back to the cottage. Charlotte excused herself and left them before the sun had set.

***

Ethel had planned a burger and chips for their last dinner, her best version of the American style. "I thought when you said chips, you meant the hard, crispy things in a bag," Chase said.

"No, no, we call those crisps. What you call French fries are chips to us," Ethel said, dishing him out another helping. "Did this disappoint you?"

"No. Ethel, I'm going to miss your cooking." Chase nodded toward Parker. "This guy couldn't cook if his life depended upon it. So, it's back to beans and steak for us. Can't ever go wrong with a steak on the grill."

Ethel's eyes widened. She washed her hands and gave each of them a hug before she left.

"Man, I'm going to miss her," Jason said.

"Me too," Parker added. "I'm going to head out and take one last walk before I head to bed." Parker grabbed his new hat and headed out the cottage door.

The night had settled, and a dainty mist fell from the sky, adding moisture to the air. Inhaling the smell of the country he would leave in the morning. He had grown attached to the laziness of it all. The riding for pleasure, the sweet smell of wet grasses rather than cow pies and dirt. He did, however, miss Blossom and his saddle. As the thought came to him, he quickly tried to brush it away; he was going to miss Charlotte.

The lights on the barn beamed through the top windows. Parker made his way there, hoping to catch Charlotte one last time. He pushed through the barn doors with little effort, closing them after. The beating of his heart quickened at the sight of her. Just as he had seen her the first time, dancing with her big brown gelding.

As much as he hated to admit it, there was a beauty in the dance created under that small flap of leather. The horse bounced in a slow, rhythmic step underneath her deep seat. The two of them flowing like waves of the ocean as horse carried his rider across the soft dirt. It gave him a new respect, but still didn't think he'd ever sit on one again.

He made his way over to the white fencing and leaned over it, clasping his hands, lacing his fingers together, and watched. Charlotte rode, unaware of the broody cowboy watching for a good ten minutes.

Squaring her shoulders, she sat back, halting the big gelding in the middle of the arena. His hooves perfectly matched in a quiet stance. The steam from his warm body flared out his nostrils like a teakettle from his workout.

"How long have you been here?" Charlotte asked. She scratched the back of her neck.

That cocky grin filled his face. "Long enough to enjoy the show."

"I need to cool him down. Walk with me?"

Parker stood up. "Yes, ma'am."

The princess dismounted and pulled the reins over the gelding's head. She led him toward the cowboy and walked through the gate he held open.

"So, is there a purpose to that sort of riding you were doing?"

"It's called Dressage. It's an old yet still ridden equine discipline. They have it in America, you know?"

"Yeah, I suppose so. I just pay little attention to the prissy stuff."

"Prissy, huh?"

Parker shrugged.

"I bet you couldn't do half of the movements. It's like military training for riders. Precise communication between horse and rider."

"Probably so," Parker agreed. "I've just got no reason to get Blossom to dance around like that. I just need her to move off my leg when I need her to. Keep pace with the cattle and hold them steady when I rope them."

"I guess that's the cowboy way, isn't?"

"It sure is. The tradition is dying. It's why Chase and I started the vlogging, to help save the ranch and show people the importance it holds in our past and our future."

"I see the value in it," Charlotte said, admiring him. Her heart ached slightly, knowing he would leave in the morning.

"I might miss this place a little." Parker stopped. His eyes met hers. "Thank you for inviting us. Giving us this opportunity to get a change of scenery. I really needed this." He gave a couple of fist pounds to his chest.

Charlotte placed her hand over his on his chest and she looked up into his chocolate brown eyes, that she had grown to love so much. "I will miss you too, Parker." The princess dropped the reins to her horse, and he took the chance to graze on the surrounding grass. Charlotte put both of her hands on either side of Parker's sandpaper skin on his cheeks and rose to her tippy toes to kiss him.

The soft mist had turned into a light rainfall as it slowly soaked the two lovers who could never be. Covering them in a watery last kiss. A kiss that melted the heart and warmed the soul from the inside out. The kiss that bonded one to another, only to be shattered again.

"Take me with you," Charlotte asked as she gently pulled away. "Please."

"Charlotte." Parker took a long sigh. "You know I can't. Your sister would send a bounty hunter after me."

The princess laughed and slapped his wet shirt. It gave a dull thud. "Let me handle her."

Cupping the soft skin of her face against his calloused hand, she leaned into him. "Thank you." He kissed her wet forehead. "For healing my heart and allowing me to know I can love again." He ducked his head to conceal any chance she would see the tear or two that escaped his eyes and walked off toward the cottage, never looking back.

Chapter 10 Home Again

Waking up in his own bed after so long was a treat. Parker had missed the smell of home, as the leather and sweaty dirt smell of his room filled his senses; a calm overcame him. He couldn't wait to see Blossom. It had been too late when they arrived the night before to visit her. He was exhausted from traveling and passed out in a matter of minutes.

After pulling on his boots and his new hat, with his saddle on his hip, he made his way out to the pasture. "Parker!" He hadn't thought to check if his dad was at his desk. "I'm glad to see you home, son. How was the trip?"

"It was eye opening for sure. Did you know they didn't use the same saddle as we did? Or was that just something I was unaware of?"

Charlie scratched his head. "Well, I suppose I sort of knew that. I just thought they would have options. Did they force you to ride in one of those?"

"Once or twice. I opted to ride bareback after a while." Charlie chuckled as Parker continued, "I see the luxury in it. It's light and gives the rider a closer feel. I just felt, well, naked on it."

"Different isn't always bad. Just depends on what you're doing, I guess." Charlie pointed a pen at his son. "I like the new hat."

"It was a gift from the princess."

"A mighty fine gift. You must have made a good impression."

"I guess you could say that," Parker replied, with a blush.

"I'm looking forward to what Jason comes up with. In the meantime, we are sure glad to have the three of you back. It's been rough missing my three best hands."

"Thanks dad." Parker knew that was as good of a compliment as he would get from his father. It surprised him he had even gone that far. "I'm off to see Blossom before we head out." He tipped his hat with his free hand and left his father to his paperwork.

Heading out to the barn, Parker set his saddle on his rack and ventured to the last place he had left his girl. He whistled a small tune as he neared the gate. Blossom's head flew up, her mane took flight and landed swiftly back on her neck as she rose from her grazing. She knew the familiar song of her favorite human. She whinnied in recognition.

"That's right, it's me. I told you I wouldn't leave you forever." Parker stopped at the gate and hung his elbows over the fence. "Well, come on. Don't you miss our rides?"

Blossom grumbled a little and swung her head as she plodded over to her master. He put a hand out flat to meet her forehead and she rubbed against him, itching. "That's my girl." Parker opened the gate and placed her head inside the halter that was hanging on the fence next to him.

Smiling, because it was good to be home, he led her to the hitching post and tied her next to Chase's gelding. "Morning Grey," he patted the big gray horse on the neck, "your partner is already up and about, huh?"

"Yup, I was up and at'em with the sun," Chase said, rounding the corner with a breakfast burrito the size of a book in one hand.

"I hope you got one of those for me."

"Of course." Chase nodded over his shoulder behind him. "It's inside the ranch house there."

"Someone was glad to be home," Parker added.

"You've no idea. It's made me realize I can be better. I mean, look getting up early, buying my boys' breakfast." Chase puffed out his chest slightly. Proud of his minor accomplishment.

"I think that's great. This new Chase is a good thing." Parker readied himself to run right before he said, "We'll see how long it lasts." He took off for the ranch house, laughing and shutting the door behind him.

"Why you no good...!" Chase yelled out before the door shut behind his friend.

Parker grabbed his burrito and checked the schedule on the front board. Looking it over, when Kyle walked in. "Hey Park. Good to have you back, my man."

Having just took a large bite of his breakfast, Parker nodded.

"What's on the schedule today?" Kyle joined Parker at the list. "Aww, I'll join with you and Chase on this first one of fifteen. I've got a three-year-old I'm training. He's been doing pretty good."

"Is that the one you had shipped down from the Dakotas from your uncle's ranch?" Parker asked between bites.

"That same one. He's coming along nice. Built like a powerhouse."

Nodding his approval, Parker finished his burrito. "There's a few more of these if you wanted one, over there on the counter."

"Thanks man, I might just help myself to one."

"Don't thank me, thank Chase. He got up early and made a decent human of himself." Parker formed quotations with his fingers.

"It won't last long," Kyle added, grabbing a burrito.

"My thoughts exactly," Parker said, and walked out the door to saddle his horse.

Chase had already saddled Blossom. "Wow, you really are on a good-guy mission," Parker stammered.

With a loud thud, Chase landed his hand on Parker's back. "Park, I've just turned a new leaf."

"Okay, my friend. I'll support you in your endeavors, you know that." Parker gently placed the bridle on his mare, but left her tied. "Just bring breakfast burritos every morning."

"Yeah, maybe if you pay every once in a while," Chase added. "Let's get these other horses saddled up before our guests arrive."

The guys saddled up twenty horses, fifteen for their ride and another five for a second ride, leaving shortly after theirs with Scott as their guide. When the larger group arrived, Kyle took them into the ranch house to sign liability waivers, and then they came out a few at a time for Chase and Parker to help match them to their steed.

Like always, Chase took the lead. Wooing the ladies of the group with his charms. "This way, my gentle ladies and men. Today we will ride across the beautiful Arizona desert. Did you know that we only get around three inches of rain a year?"

With one leg hanging over his saddle horn, so he could face the guests, he let Grey follow the path. "We have many interesting plants and creatures here in the desert that have a high tolerance for not only drought but heat. We have reached temperatures in the 120s." Chase removed his hat and fanned it at his face. "It must be the hot vibes radiating off of me."

The group laughed.

"Even though Arizona is part desert, it is one of the most diverse states. If you drive North, only just two to three hours, you'll find yourself in the middle of our pine tree forests. Where the elevation is higher. And believe it or not, gets snow!"

Kyle rode his young gelding up next to Parker, who was veering out of the horizon. "Have you ever counted how many times Chase has said this little speech?"

Parker chuckled. "No, I lost count a long time ago. I just zone out with the sound of the horses' hooves against the rocks and gravel."

"So, what do you think of this guy?" Kyle asked, lifting his reins to pull his young horse back for Parker to view.

"He is a stout little guy for a young horse. Does your uncle have any more of those?"

"He just might. I could ask him?"

"Sure. I'm always up for starting a new colt."

"Want to see him move out?"

"Yeah, but maybe not here. There's a whole lot of cholla around."

Kyle flicked his hand in a quick wave. "That won't phase this guy. Besides, a little cactus hurt no one."

"Alright, give him a go then."

Nudging the gelding on Kyle rode him ahead to the side of the train of guests. He weaved in and out of cactus at a slow trot. The young horse followed nicely, maneuvering quickly around the desert brush and cacti. Kyle was smiling from ear to ear, proud of his project pony.

"I've started him from zero. My uncle's horses are born out on the range, untouched, rounded up and send to trainers all around to break and place in new homes."

"You've done a stellar job, Kyle."

Just as Kyle asked the young gelding to swing around and join up with Blossom, he got a little too close and a small bunch of cholla cactus leaped off, attaching onto the horse's leg. He shot up straight into the air. All four hooves off the ground. Bounding from side to side as he wildly kicked his legs to relieve the stabbing pain the needles inflicted upon him.

"Stay calm folks. Your horses may get a little excited. Just keep them walking. Pull back on your reins to steady them," Chase yelled over the gasps and hollering of Kyle.

"Hold him Kyle," Parker coached. "That's it, stay with him. Bend him around!"

The horse continued to buck. Flinging his hind quarters through the air. "Maybe you should train him to buck for the rodeo," Chase bellowed out over a laugh.

After a few minutes, Kyle held his young horse steady. His legs shaking like a leaf in the wind. He cooed him gently. "Easy there, boy. You're alright, partner." When he tried to dismount, the gelding took off bucking again. This time, Kyle brought him back down quicker. "Whoa, there, buddy."

Parker got off Blossom and walked toward the shivering horse. "Let me try to get it off, Kyle. Just keep him calm." Parker held up his hands to show the young horse he meant him no harm. "Easy boy. Let me help you."

The young horse continued to shake. His wide eyes showing the whites of fear. His nostrils flared. Parker reached out to pet his neck. He recoiled slightly, but quickly calmed at the touch of Parker's hand. Parker bent down carefully, never releasing his touch from the horse's sweaty coat.

Opening his knife, Parker made a swift snake-like movement, flicking the cactus off and away from the horse's leg. The horse jumped, moving himself away from Parker. Kyle stopped him, coaxing him again. The young horse then licked his lips as he took a sigh of relief, now that his leg no longer held the needles of the cholla.

The group of guests clapped and cheered. Parker tipped his hat. "That cowboy can ride." He gestured to Kyle, still on top of his horse. "This poor horse is still learning that people can help him." He mounted Blossom who had parked herself where he left her. "That's my good girl," he said as he swung his leg over the saddle. He'd missed her so much. A sense of peace filled him as he sat in the familiar hunk of leather. It held him like a hug, comforting his soul.

"Shows over folks. There's never a dull moment in a cowboy's life." Chase nodded at Kyle, showing his approval of handling the situation so calmly. "Did you know that the Saguaro cactus only grows here in Arizona and Mexico?" Chase stopped next to a tall, slender green tower of prickles. An arm extended out to one side. "The Saguaro cactus is only found in the Sonoran Desert."

The crowd talked amongst themselves in awe of the facts. A small white bloom radiated from the tip of the arm of the cactus, delicately beaming as it protruded out from the sharp spikes. Yellow, red and purple flowers dotted the surrounding area, scattered along the trail. Prickly pear grew along the path with red fruit, giving the guests a new perspective of the beauty of the surrounding desert.

The day finished with happy customers. "Don't forget to leave a positive review," Parker yelled after them, still sitting on Blossom. He leaned slightly forward with his one arm resting on top of his boot that was crossed over the top of his saddle horn. His back muscles ached from the long day. He inhaled deeply. The dirt, the sweat of the horse beneath him, and the desert plants all gave his heart a warm peace. The thought saddened a part of him; he would never see Charlotte again. Parker bit on his bottom lip, remembering the feeling of her soft lips against his.

"Hey lover boy," Chase slapped the bottom of Parker's boot, dust puffed, "dreaming of a princess?"

"Maybe?"

"I could tell. Your face looked like a powered baby butt," Chase spouted off and made a run for it.

Parker quickly placed his leg back over Blossom's side and spun her around into a gallop after his so-called friend. "Why I otta!" He arrived too late as Chase had jumped the cattle pen and had darted off into a nearby chute, laughing so hard he almost couldn't stand.

"I love you, man!" Chase yelled out over the mooing cows.

"You no good for nothing," Parker mumbled to himself. He nudged Blossom on away from the ranch house to check on the exterior of the ranch, where they let the beef cattle roam free to get fat on the desert shrubs.

The sunset over the horizon held an orange, pink hue that settled over the purple mountains in the distance. A light haze of dust hung in the eyes-view. There was nothing like an Arizonan sunset. He checked the watering hole and walked along the fence exterior. He found no stuck or dead cattle and called it a good day.

When he arrived back at the ranch, he heard a shouting coming from the ranch house. He quickly unraveled his cinch and pulled the saddle off his mare. As he walked to the rack, Kyle grabbed his elbow. "This way." He motioned his head away from the building. "Trust me, you don't want to go in there."

"What is going on?" Parker's face drew out the question. "Is that Chase I hear yelling?"

"Yeah. He's mighty upset, too." Kyle stopped, still trying to pull on Parker to lead him away, but Parker had planted his feet. "C'mon man, please."

Parker handed his saddle to Kyle. "Put this in my room, will ya?"

Kyle slumped and let out a giant sigh. "Park, you're going to regret this."

"I can't leave my best friend, who's trying to be a better man, alone, to fight whatever battle is going on over there." Parker pointed to the ranch house. "What kind of friend would that make me?"

"Yeah, yeah. I guess. Good luck, and don't forget I warned you." Kyle shrugged and headed toward the main house with Parker's saddle in tow.

Picking up a quick pace, Parker let Blossom into her pasture and then headed for the ranch house. As he neared the door, his heart stopped. Panic filled his veins, the blood inside him turned to ice. The door swung open and a stunning, dark-haired beauty strutted out. A wicked smile spread across her face. All Parker could do was stare, frozen. His eyes glimpsed his best friend behind her. Chase grimaced. His face seemed to apologize. Chase rubbed the side of his neck, unaware of how to approach the situation he had tried so hard to avoid. He hoped Parker's ride was long enough to avoid this situation. Unfortunately, he had failed.

CHAPTER 11 BRIEL

A little boy walked up to the woman, grabbing onto her leg. Parker watched him intently. "Mama, I want to go home."

"Not right now, Garth," she said, patting his head. She turned her attention back to Parker. "You look good. How have you been, Park?"

Before answering, Parker swallowed the dry lump that had formed in his throat. It didn't budge. He rubbed the back of his damp, tingling neck, then lifted his hat to scratch his head, where there was no itch. "I've learned to cope. How are you Briel?" And there it was, the first time he had spoken to her since she had left him over six years ago. Broke his heart, shredded his pride and stomped on his spirit.

She hadn't changed. Her raven locks of hair formed waves of ironed curls down her mid-back. The tight formed bejeweled blouse shaped her attractive curves and over the large lady lumps he knew had recently been added. Her skirt was short, with a western flare at the bottom that hung above her knee. It went well with the white cowgirl boots that decorated her legs.

"Is that... Ours?" Parker motioned a shaky finger to the little boy, still whining as he tugged on her skirt. Another dry lump surfaced, almost choking him this time.

"Our son?" Briel cocked her hip to the side, her long manicured fingernails trailed over her skirt. "You aren't even man enough to say it out loud." She pulled the little boy up to her side. "You need to have a part in this. I shouldn't have to deal with this alone."

"You left me Briel. Abandoned me with no contact, no trace, nothing. You left me at the altar. I stood there waiting. Hoping," Parker choked out. "I thought you got married? And wasn't he adopted? Your dad told me..."

"I did! But he left me once he found out I had a kid. He helped me with the hospital bills and then left me!" Briel stomped her feet over to the frozen cowboy. "I lost a good husband and a fortune all because you couldn't keep your hands off of me!"

"Bri... I... I thought you loved me, like I loved you."

Briel rolled her eyes as a huff left her lips. Lips he once had kissed. Parker watched the woman in front of him, disgusted with himself that he had once loved her. How had he lost so much heartache over this hateful person standing in front of him?

"I thought you could give me a life. But I was stupid and young Park. Instead, you gave me a little boy who dragged me down. My dad lied to help you let go. So, you wouldn't feel you had to commit yourself to me. My husband has agreed to take me back if I can give you what is yours."

Parker's eyes narrowed. "What are you saying, Briel?"

"Don't try to sweeten me up! You don't have no claim to me anymore," she spat out.

"Are you saying that you'll just leave the boy here? With me?"

Rolling her eyes, she spun around as if to look around her. "I don't see anyone else standing here."

"I don't know the first thing about how to raise a kid." Parker looked at the little boy. His brown eyes reflected his own. A sadness clenched his heart for the child.

"And you think I do? Listen, take the boy, raise him to be a cowboy. He can help you run the ranch, hang out with your grouchy old dad. I don't care. Just take him. He's yours too. Take some responsibility." She set the little boy down. "Oh, and he turns six on Friday."

Without a care, she turned on her fancy white heeled boots and walked away. The little boy called after her as his little legs carried him as fast as he could muster, with ugly tears streaming down his face as he sobbed for her to wait. Briel stopped, bent down and looked the little one straight in the eyes. "Do you remember how mommy said you had to be strong like a cowboy?"

He nodded, and his hair flopped up and down as he wiped his wet cheeks with the back of his hand.

"Good. This man here is going to teach you to be a real man. He will teach you how to ride horses, and rope cows. He will teach you how to be a cowboy." Tears filled her eyes again. "I expect you to be the one to save the cowboy way."

Garth held his bottom lip out as he listened to his mom. She had told him before that someday he would have to be strong and learn how to be a tough cowboy. He just wasn't sure he wanted to do it without her. And he didn't know the strange man standing behind him. He only knew her. She was his mother.

Briel's eyes flicked up and met Parker's and for the first time that night he saw she cared. Even if she acted as if she didn't. He didn't know what had happened to her in the last several years, but she had changed. She had hardened. And he was glad that she had left him that day, because the woman he thought he had loved would never abandon their son, like she was doing now.

"Why Briel?" Parker walked toward her. "We could try again?"

She didn't even skip a beat. "No Parker. I'm going to travel. I've signed a record deal and I can't have a little person following me around. What kind of life would that give him?"

"A record deal?" Parker's eyebrow raised.

"Yeah, for country singing."

"I don't remember you being a singer."

Briel bit her bottom lip. "Well, I'm a back stage dancer if you will." She threw up a hand and turned a circle.

The car honked.

"Just a blasted minute," she yelled. "He's so impatient."

Parker only nodded. It made sense. Briel was always one for attention. Maybe this would fill that void she had always sought after. He looked down at the little boy, *his* little boy. The one he thought he had lost forever.

"I left my number for emergencies only in the ranch house. His suit case is in there too. He doesn't like tomatoes." Briel placed a hand on the top little boy's head. "Garth, you listen to Parker. He is your real daddy, ok?"

Garth peered up at the tall cowboy next to him. He frowned, still confused at why this had happened. Not understanding why, he couldn't just go with his mom. His little mind raced with possibilities. He would be a good boy for her, she didn't have to leave him.

Briel bent down and kissed his brown hair and left. Garth stood there watching the woman he called mother walk away. Leaving him with a strange cowboy. Tears streamed down his pale pink cheeks, but he didn't dare let out a whimper, because he knew he was a cowboy now, and cowboys didn't cry.

Parker just stood there watching her walk away, next to his son. His son, what a strange thought. A thought he never thought he would hear. With footsteps behind him, he turned and gave a smug smile.

Chase laid a hand on his shoulder. "I'm sorry Park. I tried to send her away before you got here. Are you ok?" Parker nodded. Even though inside, his heart was racing, his mind a fog and his stomach dry with knots. Chase looked down at the little boy. "Looks like we got ourselves a new ranch hand." He held out his hand. "Hey little man, I'm Chase, your new favorite uncle."

Stunned for a second, the little boy rubbed the tears from his cheeks, wiped them on his jeans, and took Chase's hand. "I'm Garth."

"That's a noble name. They named you for one of the world's best singers." Chase squeezed Parker's shoulder.

Parker half smiled and huffed a little. He took his son's hand; a strange tingle caused him to shiver. He had a son. A tingle of warmth accompanied his chill of doubt. "Come on, son, let's find you a room, and meet your grouchy old grandpa."

"I have a grandpa?" Garth asked, his little brown eyes seemed to sparkle through the drying tears. "And an uncle." His other fingers laced into Chases.

Chase looked over at his best friend. With a small shrug, they smiled and walked forward, leading the new little cowboy to the main house.

When they entered the house, it seemed empty. Their footsteps echoed in the tall ceilings that were lined with old oak logs. A brick fireplace was in the center of an open family room, over it hung an enormous set of longhorns. The couches were brown harness leather, soft and inviting. The only light came from a kitchen and a door that was closed. It led down a wide hallway.

The three of them walked through the family room to the closed door and knocked. "Come in," they heard a voice say on the other side. As prompted, they opened the door. Charlie sat behind a large desk, and as normal, he was working on paperwork. He peered over his readers. "What do you have here?"

"Dad, do you remember a few years back when Briel left me? And remember that tiny little detail that she had been pregnant?"

Charlie stood, pushing his chair backward into the wall behind him. He quickly swiped the glasses from his face and was at his son's side, hugging the little boy. He steadied him, giving him a look over to see familiar brown eyes staring back.

Parker looked at Chase. His eyes widened at the scene in front of him. Chase shrugged.

"Do you know who I am, young man?" Charlie asked Garth.

"No, sir."

"I am your grandpa."

"My grouchy grandpa?"

"Who told you I was grouchy?"

The little boy pointed at his new found dad. Parker held a fist to his mouth to cover the laughter that wanted so badly to escape.

"Well, I'm only grouchy to my son, who is your daddy. Because he needs a firm hand. Do you know what that means?"

"No, sir."

"It means I'm teaching my son to be strong, because growing up on a ranch means you have to work hard from sunrise to sundown. It means you have to make sure every animal is fed and safe before you eat or sleep. Being a cowboy is an enormous responsibility. Can you do that?"

Garth licked his lips. This was a big decision for him. And he didn't want to let his mama or his new daddy, grandpa or uncle down. He knew what it was like to feel hungry. Sometimes his mama had forgotten to get him dinner while she was off singing. But he was strong, and he pushed through it. He was sure that was because he was born to be a cowboy.

"Yes, sir. I want to be a cowboy." Garth straightened his shoulders and pressed his lips tight.

"Good, that's the spirit." Charlie patted the boy and stood up to look his son in the eye. "Looks like we got ourselves a new ranch hand, boys." Charlie pulled Parker aside. "I know this was a lot for you. How are you holding up?"

"I'm doing the best I can, I guess. Not that she gave me much choice."

Pulling Parker to look him straight in the eyes, a hand on each shoulder, he said, "Son, I'm proud of you. You did the right thing. We'll make a good man out of him." Charlie smiled as he examined his son. "He's got your eyes. Besides, he's better off with us than that wench. I never understood what you saw in her. Don't be upset, but I found evidence of abuse on the boy."

"What?" Parker's fists balled up. "How could she?"

"I don't know. It could have been a boyfriend." Charlie took a deep breath. "The boy is better off with us."

A tickle formed in Parker's nose as he did his best to conceal the tears that threated to form in his eyes. Not only had his dad told him he was proud, it was all, just a lot. He knew nothing about raising a kid. How was he supposed to be an example to a little boy he didn't even know? If he felt this way, how was this poor kid feeling? He didn't know how to comfort him or show him that everything was going to be ok. He knew one thing; the boy was safe now, and no one was ever going to harm him again.

Any last hopes he and Charlotte might have had to make it work were now completely gone. There was no way a princess would want to take on someone else's child. Think of the scandal that could cause with her country.

Parker didn't know how long he had been standing there, in a daze of confusing thoughts and emotions. Chase placed an arm over his shoulder and pulled him in for a squeeze. "You're not alone Park. Just don't hesitate to voice how you feel. I know you like to hold it all in."

"Thanks Chase. It's just so much, I don't even know where to start." Parker looked around. "Where's the kid?"

"Your dad took him up to the spare bedroom."

"Great." Parker nodded. "Yeah. This is going to be fine."

"Of course, it is. Look at us." Chase held his arms out to his side, like he was basking in the moonlight.

"Yeah, that's what I'm afraid of, us raising that poor kid. He's doomed."

"No way. Wait until the fans see him. He's going to be their new favorite star."

"I sure hope you're right." With that, Parker left Chase to shower and turn in for the night. It had been a long, weird day, and nothing sounded better than sleep.

CHAPTER 12 A BOY AND HIS PONY

Two months had gone by since Briel had left Garth at the ranch. She hadn't called even once. Garth had settled nicely. Learning all the things a little cowboy must do to be a good ranch hand. If he wasn't helping talk Grandpa Charlie's ear off, then he was following Chase around, learning to smooth talk to the ladies. Parker couldn't be prouder of his boy.

"Ladies," a little voice said as he tipped his hat. "Riding horses is a rough and tough job. My grandpa's grandpa ran this ranch with his *beer* hands." Garth squinted his eyes as he handed the morning trail riders their waivers. "It can be dangerous out there, so we gots to sign papers."

"Thank you, little guy. What is your name?"

"Garth," the boy pulled off his hat and held it to his chest, "and I run things around here."

"You do?" The woman handed back her signed liability waiver. "I'm impressed. Do you have your own horse too?"

Placing his hat back on his head, he pressed his little lips together in deep thought. "My daddy says I've just about earned me my own horse. I ride with him on Blossom sometimes." He held up his two small hands, five fingers on one hand and one on the other. "But see, I'm six now, and daddy says that's plenty big for a cowboy to have his own horse. I will have to brush him and feed him even."

The other lady handed her signed paper to Garth. "Thank you, ma'am. My Uncle Chase will be *em-scorting* you on your ride today. Please follow me." Garth led the two ladies to the tie area, where Chase leaned against a fence post. Proud to be the little man's father, Parker watched from a distance. A grin spread wide across his face as he observed his son act as if he was born to work on the ranch.

It was hard at first to take on the sudden surprise of, guess what? You get to be a dad and figure it out overnight. Garth was the best of everyone. Garth was strong; he tried his best to work hard, and Parker couldn't ask for a bigger blessing. He had come at the perfect time. His heart had learned to move on, thanks to Charlotte.

Parker wondered if he hadn't of had the change of heart in Europe, what reaction he would have had the night Garth came to them? Being a dad made it easier for him to forget Charlotte. He didn't have the time or energy to let his thoughts think about her when he was following around a little cowboy.

Chase took over the moment they stepped into the open corral. "Ladies, I hope you're well and ready to ride today? I see you've met our host for the day." He tipped his hat to the small cowboy. "Garth."

"Are we riding big Grey today, Uncle Chase?"

"Not today, my man. I've got this ride handled. Your dad has big plans for you today." Chase nodded toward the post where his friend still stood. His arms folded over his plaid, button down.

"Aww man. I was looking forward to taking these ladies out."

Chase placed a hand on the disappointed cowboy's shoulder. "Don't you worry. You're going to like what he has planned. Now go before he changes his mind."

The two ladies waved goodbye to their small helper, but immediately forgot once the tall, blond, flirty cowboy took over, demanding the center of all attention, as Chase always did.

Garth padded the ground as fast as his little leather boots could carry him toward his dad. "What is the hurry, little man?" Parker chuckled, watching the small boy hustle.

Stopping next to his dad and looking up just under the brim of his hat, Garth slumped his shoulders and released an enormous sigh. "I really wanted to take those pretty ladies riding today." He sighed again. Letting his dad know he was unhappy about this whole situation. "But Chase said you had plans for me. And I know," he threw his hands into the air and landed them back on his hips, "a cowboy never complains. But dad I really like riding."

"I know, Garth, and that is why we are going to take a drive."

Just as he felt he belonged; little Garth was hit with a block wall. His heart pounded; a damp warmth made his cheeks blush. He brought his hands to his face to conceal any tears that would make him weak. Make him un-cowboy-like. He had tried so hard to make his daddy proud of him. When an adult takes you on a drive, it never means good things. That is what his mom had done. He was happy here at the ranch. Why was his dad wanting to end it now?

The tears escaped down his cheeks and under his hands, which failed to conceal his emotion. "Garth?" Parker kneeled to be level with the boy. "What's the matter, son?" He pulled his slight frame into his chest, hugging him tightly. Then pulled him out to look him in the eye as his son spoke.

"I—I thought, I thought I was doing a good job as a cowboy." He sniffed.

"You are? You're one of the best cowboys ever. So why are you upset?"

Garth took his hands from his face; pink splotches patched his cheeks. His lips tightly bound, they quivered. "Mommy took me for a drive when she tired of me. Sometimes she left me in the car. It was hot. I thought I was being a good cowboy for you."

Squeezing the boy again, he said, "Garth, I'm going to make you a promise. Do you know what a promise is?" His small head nodded, the brim of his hat bumping his dads. "I promise you I will never take you for a drive like your mom did. Your mom doesn't always make great choices. This doesn't make her bad, because I know she loves you. It's just hard sometimes to be an adult and do adult things."

Parker grabbed a hold of Garth's chin to bring him eye level. "Can you make me a promise back?" The boy straightened his shoulders, taking this seriously, and nodded. "Good, I need you to help me, Chase, and grandpa run this ranch. It's vital that you help us. So, I have decided to get you your own horse, because you are part of this ranch. I've got a friend on the other end of town who's got a pony just your size, and he needs a cowboy just like you to ride him." Garth's eyes widened and his lips softened into a smile.

"Oh, I promise daddy. I'll be the best cowboy. *E-specially* with my very own horse."

Unable to keep the grin from his face, Parker grabbed the hat off his son and ruffled his hair before he placed his back on his little brown tuff. "I know you will, son. Now go get in the truck so we can go get you a pony!" Garth never ran faster than his little boots carried him in that moment.

It was a thirty-minute drive to pick up the new pony. Earl was a friend and neighbor rancher to Charlie since Parker could remember. It was smart to be friendly with the guy you shared a property line with. Parker also went to the same school as Earl's kids, but they were never buddy-buddy.

As they pulled up, Earl was working on an old tractor in front of a rugged red barn. He was bent over with his waist up inside the engine of the machine. "Hey-ya Earl!" Parker voiced after closing his truck door.

"Oh," Earl said, a touch startled as he came up from the engine a little greasy. "I lost track of time working on this ol' tractor here." Earl made his attention over to the boy. "Are you ready to meet your pony, young man?" The old man wiped his hands on his overalls, adding to the many greasy stains.

"I sure am. My daddy says I get to be a real cowboy now that I get my own pony."

"Well, I think a cowboy's first horse must be a special one. He'll be the one to teach you all the important things about being a cowpoke."

"What's a cowpoke?" Garth questioned. His little nose wrinkled at the sound of such a funny word.

"Oh, it just is another silly word for cowboy, I suppose," Earl added. "Come on, this way." He waved a hand for them to follow. "I had one of my hands put him in the barn back there." He led them through the red barn. It was full of hay and farm machines. They walked all the way through the barn turned right into another barn that wasn't as tall. It was more of a large covered mare motel.

This barn was white and stabled at least twenty horses. Garth counted, but he could only count to twenty, so he wasn't sure if there were more. "You guys have a lot of horses."

"That we do, my boy. My son, who your daddy went to school with, breeds and trains them. We've got over a hundred on the West pasture."

Garth's face lit up, his eyes squinted, then grew wide with his open mouth. "Wow! One hundred?"

"Or something like that. Y'all have an acceptable number of horses at your ranch too, last I checked."

"Yeah, we do." Parker added. "I think we are around thirty or so."

Earl led them all the way down the aisle way of horses. Some of them came to their gates to greet them, some did not. Garth eyed every single horse, hoping that one of them would be the one. They had already walked so far. Almost at the end of the mare motel, Earl stopped. He opened a gate and walked in, waiting for Garth and Parker to follow.

Inside, Parker couldn't believe his eyes. There stood a short version of a horse. "What do you think? Do you think you and this guy here could be friends?" Earl asked.

Garth pointed to himself. "Me and him?" he bit on his lip. "Yeah, I think we could be best friends."

***

When they arrived back at the ranch, Chase had just finished with his second trail ride of the day. He hustled to unsaddle the horses. After, he made his way over to the truck and trailer to greet Parker and Garth.

Jason was already filming to catch Garth lunge out of the passenger door, the moment Parker put the truck into park. Garth grinned from ear to ear. He hopped up and down at the back of the trailer door, struggling to reach for the latch that kept him from his new friend.

"See this, Jason? Inside here," Garth tapped on the metal door, "this is my new horse. He's going to help me be a real cowboy. Come on, dad!"

"I'm coming," Parker said, walking next to Chase. Parker opened the door and Garth took a giant step up. The bed of the trailer was almost half his size and to reach it was a struggle. "Careful now, pet his behind to let him know you're there and walk up and untie his rope," Parker coached his son.

"Easy boy," Garth said as he squeezed through the trailer divider and the pony. "We are going to be best buddies, you and me."

"Good." Parker observed his son, conflicted if he should get up there and help him or let him learn on his own. "Now make him back up, all the way out."

The pony attempted to turn around. Going out of a trailer backward was not something he wanted to do. He pulled on the lead rope, bringing Garth with him, lunging him off his feet ever so slightly. Garth pulled back. "No. You're going to back out."

A tingle of pride trickled inside Parker's heart. This was his son, and he could not have been more blessed. This kid was born to run this ranch one day. Every day, he woke up early. He watched Chase, Charlie, or his dad, soaking in every detail of being a cowboy like a sponge. The clients loved him and he often pulled the attention from Chase. And he was a natural with the horses.

The small pony had a brown head up to his shoulders, then a white blanket of snow covered the rest of him. Random polka-dots covered his coat in every likely area. Garth led the pony off the trailer and toward the stable.

"Now every good pony needs a name," Parker suggested. "Have you thought about what you're going to call him?"

Stopping and pulling his pony to a halt with him, Garth bit on his bottom lip. His eyes squinted, helping him in deep thought. He looked up at his dad. "I think I want to call him Rusty. Because he looks kind of like he is rusting. Like Papa's old truck."

Nodding, Parker agreed. "I like that. It suits him."

"Did you get that Jason?" Garth asked. "We need everyone to meet my new pony."

"I got it, little man."

Garth led the spotted pony right up to the camera. "Hi guys, this is my new pony, Rusty." Rusty leaned his head against the rope to search for anything that might be edible on the ground. Garth pulled up on the lead rope but failed. "He's so hungry." Grunting, he tried again. "I'll do my first ride with Rusty tomorrow. My dad says he needs to settle first. That means he's got to get used to being here in his new home."

Parker helped Garth pull the pony's head up so they could continue to take him to his stall. "Come on, buddy, let's get your new friend to his bedroom, where he can eat his dinner."

"Yeah, he's seems real hungry." With the thought, his little tummy rumbled. "Me too. I think I know how he feels." Parker chuckled at Garth.

As Chase and Jason watched, Parker and Garth walk away. Jason shut off his camera. "That kid has brought in over two hundred thousand new subscribers. The fans love him."

"He's a special one." Chase rubbed the back of his neck. "Speaking of the kid and our followers. Charlotte sent me an email the other day, asking about the boy."

"Oh? What did you say?"

"I haven't responded yet. I know Parker really liked her and she helped him to move on from Briel. It was all great timing, really. With him able to heal just in time for her to show up and drop off Garth. I'm not sure how he would have handled it if he wasn't able to heal while we were in Europe."

Jason placed his camera into its case. "He would have managed alright. He's got you and he's Parker. He always seems to manage."

"Yeah, maybe. But he's broody and holds all his feeling inside. I can only imagine that he's a ticking time bomb. Lucky for us, Charlotte deactivated it before it went off on one of us."

Zipping the bag closed, Jason looped the strap over his shoulder. "So, what are you going to tell Charlotte? I mean, not that it matters because they could never be an item with her royal family and all."

Chase chuckled. "I've been emailing her back and forth a lot recently."

"Dude. That is like breaking the bro-code."

"No. It's not like that. Since her sister was married, she's relaxed at the idea of Charlotte living a life she can enjoy. Of course, it would still involve her checking in from time to time."

"What exactly are you saying?" Jason's eyebrow raised as he looked back at Chase.

"That we've been planning her to come here as a surprise for Parker. But since Garth, she's been worried he might get back with Briel. That he might still have feelings for her. It's just really not my place."

"Good luck with that."

"I can see her concern. Travel all that way only to find out he wants to get back with his ex, who he has a kid with. I mean, that's just messy."

Jason laughed. "We could video it. Would make for some great content." Chase punched Jason's shoulder. "Ouch."

"Briel isn't coming back. And what if this gives Parker a chance to find love again?"

"You're sounding all sappy dude," Jason grimaced, "be careful meddling in someone else's love life, that's my advice. Honestly, tell the princess to move on. She doesn't need that kind of drama in her royal life."

"I just want Parker to be happy." Chase sighed, pulled his hat off, and ran his fingers through his hair. "They've kept in contact with one another, so it's not just me she talks with. We were just trying to surprise him."

"I get it. I want Parker happy too. He's got Garth now. No princess wants that kind of burden. Besides, Parker isn't one for big surprises. Run it by him first."

"Yeah." Chase grumbled to himself. "You're probably right. I'll see you tomorrow, my-man."

"Yup, same time as always. Hey, I'll grab breakfast on my way in."

With a flick of his wrist, he waved Jason off. What in tarnation was he going to tell Charlotte now? That she shouldn't come? Was Parker too preoccupied with his son to worry about a princess? Why did he let himself get into these situations? He needed to find a woman of his own, no less help Parker fix his messy situation. Maybe it was him that needed Parker to help meddle in his love life.

The next morning Garth came running into his dad's bedroom, dressed in his jeans, boots and cowboy hat. He lunged onto his dad's bed, bouncing up and down. "Dad, get up!"

Groggily, Parker turned to the clock that sat on his nightstand next to his bed. "Garth, buddy, please stop bouncing the bed."

"Sorry daddy."

"Hey, it's like four in the morning. I think you beat the sun."

"Nope, it's up already." Garth beamed. He ran over to the window and threw the curtains open. "See?" The sun had just begun its ascent, barely. The sky still resembled dawn. The light was just peeking through the night's blanket.

Knowing that Garth was excited to ride his pony. Parker took in a long breath. "All right, give me ten minutes to get ready?" He threw the covers off him and sat up. He rubbed the sleep from his eyes, though it didn't seem to help much.

"A fast ten minutes, ok?" Garth jumped off the bed. "I'm going to go wake up Papa."

"No!" Garth stopped in the doorway. "Let grandpa sleep until his alarm goes off. He will come out when he's ready. That will give you time to practice with Rusty first."

"You're so smart, dad."

"I know." Parker lovingly nudged him with a soft fist bump to his cheek. "Now go, so I can get ready." He watched the little boy skip off with an extra bounce to every step.

Once Parker was dressed and ready for the day, he found Garth sitting on the boot bench by the front door of their house. His cheeks squished beneath his hands with his elbows on his knees. He waited. His little legs were too short to reach the ground, and he was swinging them back and forth; humming a country tune.

Not able to conceal a grin, Parker cleared his throat. Garth's head popped up, like a rattlesnake striking for protection. "You ready buddy?"

"Yes, sir!"

The two of them walked out the door across the yard and headed toward the stable. They haltered the spotted pony, and Parker guided the boy in wrapping his cinch, and together they buckled the breast collar. Garth wasn't tall enough to place the bridle on the pony's head, so Parker helped. Pulling the reins, Garth led his pony into the arena that Kyle had freshly turned up with the tractor the day before.

"Ready for a boost?"

"No, dad I got this," the little cowboy said, holding his hand up to stop his father from helping him. Even though Rusty was a pony and he was half the size of the full-sized horses; the stirrup still hung against the pony's side eye level with Garth. There was no way he was going to get his foot that high. Parker sat back and watched as the small boy assess his plan.

Glancing around, Garth spotted a ragged old watering bucket. He ran over to it and dragged it toward his pony. He stepped on top of it so he could get his knee into the stirrup. His foot was still too much of a stretch. Using all his might, he grabbed hold of the fender and pulled his body until his foot could replace his knee. He swung his other leg up and over the saddle. His face beamed, and when his eyes met his dad's, he smiled.

"Well done, dude," Parker praised, patting his kid on the knee. Parker let Garth ride the pony around the arena for about an hour as he gave a few instructions to work on. "I think you're ready to help me take a few customers out today? Would you like that?"

"On my own?

"Yup. I'll ride Blossom and you ride Rusty. You've got your own horse now, so you'll need to ride him, brush him, feed him, and make sure he stays healthy. Can you do that?"

"Of course, Dad. I'm a cowboy, remember?" Garth shook his head back and forth. How could his dad not realize he was a big cowboy now?

Nodding. Parker agreed, "Yes, son, you sure are." He gave the boy a quick nod with the brim of his hat.

Chase was saddling the horses for the day's trail ride when Parker and Garth came around to the front of the ranch. Peeking over the back of the horse he was cinching up, Chase called out, "Hey looking good up there, cowboy!"

"Did you see me riding him, Uncle Chase? I even got on him all by myself."

"You know only the best of us can." Chase walked around the horse and came up to Garth and Rusty. "He sure is a handsome pony." Cupping his hand to his mouth, Chase whispered, "We need to make sure he gets lots of treats." The pony's left ear flicked backward, as if he understood they were trying to hide talking about snacks.

Taking a deep breath to compose his thoughts, Chase left Garth on his pony and walked over to Parker, who headed to get Blossom from the pasture. "Hey Park, can I talk to you a sec?" he asked as he quickened his pace to catch up.

"Sure?"

"Have you talked to Charlotte since we've been back?"

"Yeah, here and there. Why?"

Chase rubbed the back of his neck. "No reason, really. I just thought maybe you guys had some chemistry. You know, back when we were there."

Keeping his face straight, Parker only allowed both his brown eyes to glance over at Chase. What was he up to? He knew better than to try to mettle in his love affairs. And now that he had Garth, he had no time for a relationship. "What are you getting at?"

"Well, I just thought maybe it would be fun to invite her to the ranch. I think she had mentioned she wanted to come check it out?"

This time, Parker stopped to look his friend in the eye. "Listen, I liked Charlotte. I mean, what is not to like? She's beautiful, but she's a princess, so it can never work between us. I can't waste my time with a woman I can never be with when I have Garth. He needs me. I will never abandon him like his mother did."

Bringing a new woman into his life just wasn't something Parker could do to Garth. The poor kid had been through a lot. He needed stability. He needed consistency, and the ranch had given him that. Being a father was new to him and he just couldn't add something else.

Nodding in agreement, Chase said nothing. He only walked next to Parker. He watched him as he called his mare and haltered her. Debating on if he should tell him he had been talking with Charlotte or not. It may send Parker over the edge. "Did you tell her about Garth?"

"She sees him in all of our videos now," Parker closed the gate after Blossom walked through, "it's not like she doesn't know."

"I just thought there was more communication between the two of you."

Parker hung his head back to sigh at the sky. "I just can't go through the heartache again, Chase. My son needs me to be strong. I can't bring a woman into his life until I know for certain she won't break him, like his mother did. He's too young to deal with that crap."

"No, you're right." Chase nodded. "I'm sorry. I only wanted to help."

"I know Chase. I know you'll always be there for me and Garth when we need you." Shoulder bumping his friend, Parker grinned. "So, what about you? What woman has caught your eye recently?"

Scuffing a boot to kick a nearby rock, Chase blushed. "Aww, you know me."

"Am I sensing something more than the normal flirty one-night stand from you?" Parker raised an eyebrow. Chase shuffled. Parker tied Blossom in her normal spot next to Grey before retrieving his saddle. "You met someone. I can tell because you're speechless."

"Well maybe. The other day, we took these two ladies out on a ride. I ended up asking one of them on a date. One date turned into three dates. I think I might like her, like more than the normal. I just didn't want to have a girlfriend and leave you behind. And it's been so long since I've actually liked a lady. I'm not even sure how to act."

"Don't worry about me, Chase. I'll be fine. I'm a big boy. Besides, I got Garth now." He nodded his head toward his kid, who was riding the spotted pony through the cattle pen while Jason filmed. "I'm happy for you. I hope this one works out for you."

"That kid is going to save this ranch."

"He's something, isn't he?"

"He was a blessing, for sure." Chase mounted his gray gelding and trotted off to join the small cowboy in the cattle pen. "Hey don't take all the spot light little man. Let me and Grey get some action on the camera."

Parker shook his head, amazed and content with how his life had turned out. Happy to have Chase as his adopted brother and a son he could say he was proud of.

Chapter 13 She Talks Funny

Garth was up extra early every morning to help Kyle feed the animals. He had to make sure that Rusty got his hay, too. Parker was in the ranch house when the little man busted through the door. "Dad!" His little chest heaved in and out. "Kyle let me drive the hay truck, and it was so hard to turn the wheel."

"He did?" Parker chuckled, knowing that the steering wheel on the truck was half his size and had little to no power steering. It was an old flatbed truck they only used for chores around the ranch. "Did you crash into anything?"

"Well, I almost ran over a cow, but I honked the horn and he ran away."

"Lucky for that cow, he was fast," Parker teased.

"Yeah," Garth breathed out, and wiped his forearm across his brow. "Ranching sure is hard work." Garth climbed onto the table next to the schedule his dad was looking over.

The door opened and Chase walked in with an armful of breakfast sandwiches. "Food is here." He placed it all on the table and Garth dove in. He unwrapped the first sandwich he could find and stuffed his mouth. "Easy little man."

"Ranching is hard work, Uncle Chase, and I'm starving."

"I'm glad I could be of service," Chase said, unwrapping his own breakfast. "So, what's the plan for today?"

"I'm going to take this first bunch of ten out with Kyle. If you want to hang back a bit with Garth. Help him saddle up Rusty. There is a group of three the two of you can take out after lunch."

"How does that sound, Garth? Want to hang out with your awesome uncle?"

"Yeah!" Garth almost growled, as he jumped off the table. His little boots pounding the floor and puffing with dust. "I got to get my hat. I left it in the hay truck." And he ran off.

Parker left Chase in the ranch house to saddle up Blossom and three other horses and met Kyle in the tie area. He had already grabbed three horses and was brushing them off. "I heard you let my kid drive without his license."

"Yup, got to teach him all the good things while he's young," Kyle teased.

"Yeah, yeah, just don't teach him anything about girls yet."

"Hah! I'll leave that up to Chase."

Parker chuckled, leaving Kyle to finish as he greeted the group that pulled up in a compact car. "Howdy there, friends. Are you here for the nine o'clock ride?"

Like most city folk who came to the ranch to get the cowboy experience, their clothes and boots were freshly picked from the store: big flashy belts with sparkly gems, pink boots with bright blue jeans tucked in. The best part was that the three of them were matching. Parker pulled off his hat and scratched his head, sniffing in a laugh that he knew would be rude.

"We are your biggest fans," one of them said. "This is Cathy, I'm Joey, and this is Rena."

"It's great to see you guys come out. Have any of you ridden before?"

"Once I rode a pony at a fair in a little circle," Rena added.

Parker placed his hat back on his head, adjusting it just right. "That counts. If I can get the three of you to head on into the ranch house to sign a waiver, then we can be off."

"Are you and Chase taking us out today?" Cathy asked.

"Kyle and me will take you guys out this time."

"Aww man, I have like the biggest crush on Chase," Joey said, bending his knees and bouncing up and down like a middle schooler.

Parker laughed. "Who doesn't?"

"Right! He's so Rico Suave," Joey swooned.

"Yeah, we could all learn a thing or two from Mr. Chase."

"This is so cool," Rena said, handing their waivers to Parker. "Is Garth around? He is my favorite, and Rusty too. Can I ride him?"

"Rusty is Garth's personal horse. I'm not sure he would want to share. He will need him to take out the group of riders with Chase later."

"Come on, let's get you three paired up with a mount."

With Kyle's help, they matched the three riders with a horse and left for the trail.

***

Chase helped Garth saddle Rusty and opened the gate to the cows. "Just push those cattle out to the pasture, little man. Don't get too close. They can kick your pony."

"Oh! I won't let them kick my pony. I'll kick them back."

"Just slap your leg and tell them 'get' if they won't move."

Rusty was a good ranch pony. He did as the boy asked, trudging behind the cows to push them out to pasture. Chase closed the gate and walked around to hop in the ranch truck and drive to open the far gate that would allow the cattle to get out to the desert to graze on the wild brush.

"Excuse me? Are you Garth?" a woman's voice asked.

Irritated that some stranger had the audacity to walk this far back into the ranch, he spun Rusty around to glare at her. "Who is asking?"

The woman raised her hand. "Hi, sorry. I'm looking for Parker or Chase."

"How did you know my name?"

"I have watched your videos many times."

"Yeah. I guess I'm famous." Garth sat a little taller on his pony.

"You are to me. And your pony is far cuter in person too. May I pet him?"

"I don't think I am supposed to talk to strangers. And you talk funny."

"I talk funny?" the woman questioned.

"Yeah. You say things weird." Garth scrunched up his little nose and narrowed his eyebrows. "I can't trust funny talkers."

The woman chuckled. "Well, in that case. Let me talk to your father."

"How do you know who my father is?" Garth narrowed his eyes. "I have to go, lady. Chase is calling me to push the cows to the far pasture. You might have to find my papa."

"Garth!" Chase yelled from the next pasture over. "Push those cows."

"Oh, let me come with you. I can just talk with Chase. That's even better."

Garth held up his hand to stop the woman. "I think that's a bad idea, lady."

"Oh bother. I can handle myself, young man."

Shaking his head back and forth, he spun his pony back around and kicked him into a trot toward Chase. He needed to tell Chase about this crazy lady as soon as possible. Who was she to think she could just barge into the cattle pen and talk to him? She was just like every other person who watched their channel. They all thought being famous meant they were just automatically friends with everyone.

"What were you doing back there, buddy? The cows have wandered. You're going to have to gather them back up."

"I'm sorry, sir. There was this lady who talked funny back there. She wanted you or daddy."

Chase pressed his lips into a thin line. "Talked funny? Like how?"

"She just sounded weird."

That's when it hit him. There was no way, right? Could it be? Would she come that far without making solid plans? "Was this lady a pretty lady?"

Garth shrugged. "I guess so. She wasn't an ugly lady. She was a pushy lady."

And then he saw her, jogging along the pasture fence. Brown hair tied back in a ponytail. Her jodhpurs shaping her delicate figure, her black boots that rose to her knees, all followed by a white button-down shirt. "Charlotte?"

"Chase," she huffed out from the short run she had just encountered. "It's so hot here." She huffed again. "How do you guys do it all day long?"

"Charlotte. How did you…? I thought we were going to plan this out?"

A big pouty lip formed on Garth's face. He then blew out his cheeks and let out a loud breath of air. "You know this lady?" he asked Chase.

"Yeah. Garth, this is Princess Charlotte. Remember the videos we watched with your dad?"

"Oh—Yeah, I guess I remember her. She doesn't look the same."

Walking up next to the spotted pony, Charlotte held out her hand. "Nice to meet you, young lad."

Feeling apprehensive about taking her hand, Garth quickly glanced at Chase for approval. Chase nodded to the boy. Garth then met the princess' hand. "Lovely to meet such a famous cowboy," she told him.

Garth tipped his hat, just like his father did. A warmth filled in Charlotte's bosom. He was no doubt his father's son. "Is Parker not around?"

"He's out on a trail ride with some customers." Chase closed the gate once Garth and Rusty had finished pushing the cattle through. "Good job. Charlotte and I will meet you back at the tie area, ok dude?"

"Ok Chase," Garth said, as he trotted his pony away.

"How was your trip?" Chase asked.

"Long and tiring."

"Do you have some place to stay?"

"I do. Thank you for asking. Mary made sure they stationed me off the ranch and escorted."

Chase walked up to the hay truck and patted her cab. "Hop in. I'll drive us back."

Charlotte held her breath as she climbed into the passenger side of the most disgustingly dirty truck she had ever encountered. "How is this truck even functioning?"

Reaching forward to pat the dash board Chase smiled. "This trusty old truck has been on this ranch for over twenty years." He peeked over at her. Her face looked as if she might vomit. "She might be long overdue for a bath."

Her narrowed eyes said it all. The white in her knuckles as she held onto the side rail of the door told Chase she was used to the finer things of life. The ranch was going to be a rude awakening for her. She was a pampered princess, after all.

When they arrived back at the ranch house. Chase parked the truck around the side and looked over at the petrified princess. "Think you can survive this dirty ranch?"

"I'm not quite sure yet." Charlotte held the back of her hand to her forehead. "I've never encountered such dry air before. I think I may be a bit faint," Charlotte griped. "Maybe, could you grab David? I may return to my room, catch up on sleep and come back tomorrow?"

"Yeah, sure thing. Let me help you out." Chase assisted the princess out and David was at their side in an instant. "David, my man. Good to see you, brother."

"Chase." David gave a quick nod of his head. "This is… An interesting place here, you call home."

Nodding as he looked around, feeling a sense of peace, Chase realized he never thought of it that way. "Can I get you guys some water for the ride back?"

"No, No." David helped Charlotte to the rental car. "I'll just get the princess back to our hotel. I think she's rather spent from the long travel."

Chase watched them drive away as Parker rode up with the three guests and Kyle. He bit on his lip, and hung back his head. Why was he always dealing with Parker's crap? He rubbed at his head under the brim of his hat as he tried to figure out what he was going to say or not say. Part of him thought maybe it would be best to just not tell Parker. That way, he wasn't meddling at all. He would just play the innocent guy.

"Hey, guys, how was the ride?"

"Oh, my gosh! It's Chase!" Joey exclaimed, almost bouncing off his horse.

This was a new one. Chase had never seen a group of guests who had matching outfits. No less pink and sparkly. This would be the perfect distraction to forgetting about Charlotte's surprise visit. He just had to make sure Garth said nothing about the lady who talked funny. "Hey Garth, can you run over and make sure I locked the gate? I can't remember."

"Sure thing, Uncle Chase."

With that, he watched the young cowboy trot off, hoping it would give him enough of a distraction to forget the whole encounter. Parker dismounted, his eyes showing his overwhelmed state. In seconds, Chase knew why. Rena, Cathy, and Joey, where all over him, touching and talking non-stop.

Parker hid by busying himself with unsaddling the horses. His eyes only peeking over the back of the horses to enjoy the pestering that he had involuntarily dumped on Chase. It was his turn to entertain. Looking back to thank his friend, Chase walked the three guests to the ranch house to sign their new cowboy hats and then send them on their way home.

CHAPTER 14 SMOOTH BUTTER

The next morning, Parker was up early. He had even beaten Garth out of bed. He peeked in the boy's room to find him sleeping soundly and decided not to wake him.

It was hay delivery day. A semi-truck load of hay was expected around six and he needed to have the hay barn cleared out and ready when it arrived.

Parker jumped into the tractor. It was much faster scraping the area clean with the bucket of a machine than by a handheld shovel. He sorted through any broken pallets and then set them all down for the first load of hay. Pallets helped keep the hay off the ground so it didn't spoil. Chase arrived just as he finished placing the last wooden pallet down.

"I asked Jason to come film today."

"For stacking hay?"

"Yeah, I think the viewers are going to love it. Take off your shirt."

"Say what?" Parker grimaced and shook his head back and forth. "No man, that's just… Weird."

"Trust me. Keep your hat, jeans, and boots on. It's only a shirt. Besides, it's hot out here. And your shirt is already nasty; wet with sweat."

"It helps keep me cool."

"Take. It. Off."

"Sheesh fine." Jason was just in time to film. To appease his friends, Parker took the shirt off slowly, swinging his hips back and forth. Chase Whistled. Once the shirt had lifted over his head to reveal the chiseled, sweaty muscles underneath, he swung the shirt around over his hat like a rope. He took off running, and whipping the shirt at Chase's behind.

A little whimper like sound escaped from Chase as he hopped around, with Parker following him. Snapping the shirt into his friend's backside repeatedly. The two of them were unaware they were being watched by a princess and her escort. Jason was still filming, but too busy laughing at his friends to notice the onlookers.

The semi-truck arrived shortly after and unloaded the stacks of hay. They used a small squeeze truck, which is like a hay forklift, to bring the bales into the barn. Chase and Parker piled a quarter of one stack on the hay truck for feeding the next few days. Sweat glistened as it rolled over the muscle bumps on their bronzed skin. With each bale weighing around one hundred pounds, they didn't need a gym when they had one in their own backyard. Together, they swung each bale up and over with no effort.

Charlotte watched from afar. Never leaving the comfort of her air-conditioned car. "Your highness, are you sure your sister would approve of this—whatever this nonsense these cowboys are doing?"

"I don't care what my sister thinks. The view is delightful."

"I'm sure you think so, but I'm not sure as your escort, if this is appropriate."

"They're clothed, for heaven's sakes, David. Stop being jealous."

"Madam!"

"Oh, stop it." Charlotte rolled her eyes. "You know, you could never have abs like those two do. I mean, look at them, they are the epitome of a cowboy super models. And not just one of them, it's both of them! This is the best thing I've seen in a long time, so shut your mouth."

David, insulted, folded his arms over his chest. He was speechless. "Well, I…" He looked out his window away from the hay barn and Charlotte, and pouted.

"You can leave anytime. I came here to escape the snobby ways of back home. I want to live. I don't want to worry what others think. If you can't accept that, you can just go home. I'll be fine without you."

Charlotte opened the car door and stepped out. Not caring what David or her sister thought. She needed to talk to Parker. He was the real reason she had come this far. So, she made her way toward the sweaty cowboys. "You boys need a hand?"

The sound of her voice pierced through Parker like a dagger. His heart, already pumping from lifting so many hay bales, stopped. Emotions of all kinds blasted him, sending spots to his vision, and fog to his mind. What was she doing here? Was she even real? Or was this his imagination playing tricks because he had overworked in the heat? Heat exhaustion was a real thing in Arizona.

Typical Parker, kept swinging hay bales. Brooding over that fact that she might be there. What was he supposed to say to her? He had tried to move on from the feelings he had for her. He thought he had, but his pounding heart felt otherwise. All those moments they spent together came crashing back to his memories the second he saw her. Her dark brown hair highlighted her deep blue eyes, and the pink of her lips practically begged him to jump off the truck and kiss them.

Charlotte stood next to the truck with her hands on her hips. The disgusting truck she had to take a shower after riding in the day before. "Hey Charlotte," Chase said after wiping sweat from his brow with the back of his arm. "Fancy seeing you here." He landed a quaint, innocent smile.

"I wanted to see the famous ranch for myself. Maybe I could talk one of you into taking me out on the trail?"

Chase looked over at Parker for an answer. "You mean that guy?"

"Preferably, that guy. Did he forget how to talk?"

"I'm standing right here, you know?" Parker added, with a smug face. "I hadn't planned to go out today. There is too much work on the sidelines for me to get done."

"I came all this way and you can't make time to take me on an hour ride?" Charlotte's tone was snarky. Chase's stance shrunk a little. He patted his friend on the back, the sound snapping against his damp sweaty skin. Chase looked at his wet hand, grimaced, and then wiped it off on his jeans.

It took Parker a few moments to respond, not sure how to. He rubbed at his chin and shifted from one boot stance to the other. "Charlotte." He rubbed his sweaty neck. He walked closer to her. "I don't even know where to start. I'm just not the guy that deserves to be pursued by someone like you."

"Someone like me?" Charlotte's eyes narrowed. "What is that even supposed to mean?"

"I'm going to let the two of you sort this out," Chase said, jumping down from the hay truck. "I'll be close by if you need me."

Parker scratched under the brim of his hat, lifting it slightly off kilter. "Well crap. I never make the words come out right." He sighed. "Listen, it's not you, it's just me. I don't know how to have a relationship. I screwed up the last one I had. And now I have got a kid to raise. You don't need that kind of baggage being royalty and all."

"Why does everyone think they can tell me how I feel?" Charlotte shook her head, trying to contain her anger. She could feel the blood boiling inside of her. "You're right, Parker, someone like me could never have feelings for someone like *you*. I was a fool to think so!" She spun on her heels and stormed past the rental car with David sitting in it.

Once he realized the princess was leaving without him, he put the car into drive and slowly followed her at a respectful distance, giving her time to let off some steam. He knew all too well that Charlotte had a horrible temper.

"That didn't go well at all," Chase said, startling Parker as he walked around a stack of hay.

"Hey! I thought you'd left?"

"I did, sort of. I mean, where am I supposed to go? And besides, I thought you might need me to back you up." Chase stuck a piece of hay in his mouth and leaned against the truck. "Clearly, you needed me here because you totally jacked that up."

"I'm an idiot, aren't I?" Parker squatted down to rest on his toes and covered his face in his hands. Then rubbed his temples.

"Don't need me to tell you that," Chase stated. He sucked in both lips and then released them to make a pop sound.

Jumping down from the bed of the truck, Parker growled. "Why do I have to mess everything up?"

"Listen Park," Chase took his friend by the shoulder to look at him square. "I get where you're coming from. Your heart is in the right place. You care for her and you care for Garth, and you're just afraid to let your heart open to both of them."

"It just never goes smooth for me, Chase."

"Life normally isn't a smooth stick of butter. You know this. It's more like an onion that has to be cut just right. Cooked with that smooth butter to reach that perfect temperature to reach sweetness." Chase dropped his hands from Parker's shoulders. "You still have time to make it right, if you want to."

"Do you think I should?" Parker growled out loud. His mind traveled in so many directions, he couldn't even think straight.

"It never hurts to try, my friend. And if you fall again, you've got me and Garth, who will love you no matter what. Even if you can't win over the princess. What have you got to lose?" Chase shrugged.

With a pat on Chase's shoulder, Parker said, "Thanks, man. I love ya too." He took off in a sprint in the direction the princess stormed off.

Parker ran his boots under him, pounding on the red gravel. His spurs sang a clink-clang, clink-clang, and every step left a small dust trail. The afternoon sun warmed his bare skin, and it felt sticky from the sweat. His lungs complained and tightened the more distance he covered. He considered himself to be in decent shape, but running was something he hadn't conditioned for.

When the car came into view, following a short distance behind the princess. He called out to her. She didn't hear him. Parker sped up, pushing past the car. He looked at David in the car, catching an angry glare from him as he ran by. He shrugged him off and tried again. "Charlotte. Wait."

Charlotte turned to see the half-naked cowboy running behind her. Rolling her eyes and exhaling loudly with a soft growl, she kept walking. "Go away Parker!"

"Please, Charlotte. I'm an idiot."

This made her stop. If the prideful, broody cowboy admitted he was stupid, she would allow him to explain himself. She turned and waited for him to catch up. She held one hand on her cocked hip.

Out of breath, Parker bent over, heaving his chest, and catching himself with his hands on his knees. "Give—me—one, sec." He held up one hand, waving it as he spoke. After a few seconds, he stood upright.

Silently admiring the glistening bronze skin of the perfectly chiseled man in front of her, Charlotte licked her lips. There was not one ounce of misplaced anything about Parker. He was gorgeous. His broad muscled chest veered down into a six-pack of bumpy abs. The shiny buckle and worn leather belt on his dirty blue jeans hung low on his hips.

Lifting his hat from his sweat drenched head of hair, Parker brought it to his chest. "Charlotte, I'm sorry. I know you have traveled a long way. And I was stupid not to ask you why. I just assumed you… well, I don't' even know what I thought. I just never thought a dirty, broken cowboy like me could ever win over a perfect princess like you."

"Parker…"

"No, let me finish." Charlotte nodded and Parker continued. "Going to Europe was not something I wanted to do. That was all Chase. I've been sitting here going day by day, pouting like an overgrown baby. I had my mind set to just let myself grow old and alone. Running this ranch until I shriveled into the dust, we founded it on." He brought his hat back to its place on his head. "But you, you healed something inside of me. Awakened something I never thought could come alive again. If you can look past all of that, and accept me and my boy, then I would take a chance."

Charlotte tried to speak again, but he held up his hand to stop her. "But you have to promise me we won't bring you down, or cause you any social or political damage, because you are a princess. I don't want to be the one to bring you down or make your sister upset with you. Because I'm a package deal with the boy, so you'll have to take on not one ornery cowboy, but two."

Rubbing her lips together, doing her best to keep the tears from rolling down her cheeks, Charlotte rushed into the sweaty cowboy. She wrapped her arms around him and stuck her face into his damp neck. "I'm sorry I'm a little sweaty," he said.

"Shut up and hold me, you dumb cowboy."

"Yes, ma'am," Parker said, as he wrapped his arms around her familiar frame. He had missed her so much. He hadn't realized it until he saw her next to the truck. Now holding her in his arms, he never wanted to let go. He pulled away only a little to bring her lips to his, soft; tenderly moving with hers. His body tingled and sparked as her hands slid to his bare chest. The warm touch of her skin over his round pectoral muscle, skin to skin, was almost his undoing.

"Stay," he said, a small breath over her lips.

"Yes," she replied. "Teach me."

"Whatever you want." His hands now roamed to her backside, over the feminine curves that drove him so crazy.

"Take me on a trail ride now."

Parker pulled her back from his face to look her in her eyes? "Right now? It's hot. Are you sure?"

"Yeah, I'm sure."

"Let me grab my shirt."

"You don't have to," Charlotte blushed, "grab your shirt."

Parker spun, doing a couple poses with his arms flexed, the muscled bulged, and veins popped from his work out stacking hay. "You like me shirtless, huh?" Her face turned another shade of red. "No, really, I would do that for you, but I don't want to get burned.

And the mesquite trees on the trail will rip me to shreds."

A big, pouty lip curled out under Charlotte's upper lip. "I guess, if it helps protect your baby skin."

Parker chuckled. "You just had to find a reason to baby me. Just you wait and see the thorns on those trees." He reached out a hand to her and their fingers intertwined. "Come on, let's go meet Garth."

The pretty princess had a lot to learn about the desert. It was hot, brutal, and there were a lot of plants and critters that weren't friendly.

Chapter 15 Learn to Love the Saddle

Parker and Charlotte walked hand in hand over to the tie area where Kyle had helped Garth saddle up Rusty. He sat on his pony, trying to figure out his rope. Over and over, he tried to uncoil the stiff cords. "Can I help you with that, son?"

"Oh, hey dad. Yeah, this rope just doesn't want to listen to me today."

"Remember how I told you to start at the hondo, then try to circle it around?" Parker took the rope from Garth. "If you make the circle too big, it won't coil around nicely." Parker made the rope into a round shape. "About this big."

Handing the rope back to Garth, he gathered the rope into several coils and added it to the strap on his saddle. "I really wanted to make it go fancy for our next ride." Garth looked over to see his dad holding hands with the lady with the weird voice. "Hey why are you holding her hand? Is she lost?"

Parker rubbed his cheek and looked at the pretty princess next to him. "Garth, this is a friend of mine, Charlotte. We are trying something out."

"Trying what out?"

"You don't miss a thing, do you?"

"Huh," Garth said, confused.

"Would you want to join us on a trail ride, buddy?"

"I was going to go with Kyle, but I guess he'll be fine on his own. I would rather go with you."

"Good, then it's settled. Will you go gather up Rosie while I go get the saddles?"

"Is she the big red one that bosses the other horses around?"

"That's the one," Parker confirmed.

"I thought the guests couldn't ride her?"

"Charlotte, here is a special case." Parker lifted her hand and smiled at her.

"Should I be worried?" she asked, lifting an eyebrow.

"No. She is a nice mare. She just can be a little bossy, so she needs a rider with experience."

"Great." Charlotte watched Parker walk away to retrieve the saddle and followed Garth to the pasture. "That's a mighty fine pony you're riding."

"Thanks. Only I get to ride him. He is my horse."

"I have a horse like that back home where I live, too. Only I ride him. He's my special buddy."

"Why didn't you bring him, then?" Garth asked.

"I live a long way away. We would have to ship him on a boat or fly him on an airplane. I want to make sure this is where I want to stay before I brought him all the way over."

"Hmm. That's weird," Garth said. "Rosie's halter is on that post. She's the big red one over there in the corner."

Charlotte grabbed the halter, let herself in the gate, and grabbed the mare. She led her out of the pasture, shooing away the other horses, and followed Garth back to the tie area. Parker was saddling Blossom as they approached. "She's more beautiful in person than on camera."

"Thank you. I'll have to let you ride her sometime."

"I would love that." Charlotte ran her hand over the hunky saddle that sat on Blossom's back. "There is a lot of leather here. I guess I can see why you felt so strange in an English saddle." She giggled a little to herself, remembering how awkward the cowboys looked on the hunt.

Parker walked around his mare to face Charlotte. "Yeah, these saddles here are just better suited for ranch work. More options."

"I suppose I can see your point. I'll try not to stick my nose too far up and ride in it."

Parker swooped in and grabbed Charlotte by the waist. He dipped her over and kissed her lips. She pretending not to like it, by lightly swatting him away. "Parker, everyone is watching," Charlotte said, blushing.

"At this ranch we ride western, so you're going to get over that. And every time you complain, I'm going to kiss you, even if it's in front of customers."

"You wouldn't?" She rubbed the back of her neck to relieve some of the heat that had formed there.

Parker held up his hand to stop her. "No. You asked me to teach you. So that's what I'm gunna do." A giant grin surfaced across his handsome face. "And if it means you get to be kissed, then by jolly, I don't care who sees."

Garth laughed. "I think you should make him mad again," the little boy teased.

Charlotte was not pleased with Parker's way of teaching. Part of her wanted to hide, the other part of her liked it. She enjoyed kissing him, but not in front of any audience. She would get him back. "Fine." She stepped into the stirrup of Rosie's saddle. "I'm ready. Where to?"

Reining Rusty toward the open desert, Garth took the lead. Leaving Parker to hustle to get Blossom's bridle on and still mount her. He caught up shortly with a small trot. "So, how long have you been in Arizona?"

"Three days," Charlotte answered, turning her head slightly to help project her voice behind her. "We came to the ranch the other day, but you weren't around. That's when I met Garth here."

"Yeah. That's when I knew she talked funny."

"Garth!" Parker reprimanded from the back of the line. "Tell the lady you're sorry. That wasn't a nice thing to say."

"I'm sorry Miss Charlotte."

"It's quite all right. I'm sure to a little boy my accent does sound funny." Charlotte shifted in her weight from side to side. "This saddle isn't as bad as I had once thought."

Parker only nodded, knowing that soon she would enjoy his saddles as much as she did her own. It wasn't a matter of who was better; it was the time spent on the horse. The peace and quenching satisfaction it brought to the soul. Horses had been the only thing to keep his mind sane after Briel. With Charlotte, he could feel the change in his heart. It was slowly mending and bringing down the walls that guarded his heart.

"We are coming up to the river crossing. Whatever you do, do not let your horses stop in the water. Unless you want to take a swim," Garth informed them.

"Thank you, Garth." Charlotte looked back over her shoulder as Parker came to her side. "You've taught the young man well. You should be proud."

"He's going to run this ranch one day. I expect him to know it all." Parker eased Blossom into the water. "When we take him out on trails now, he leads. I always make sure another hand is with him. He's learned all his people's charms from Chase."

"I can see why he's quickly become a star."

"He really has. If it hadn't of been for the money we got from the trip, we could have lost the ranch. With Garth here running the show, we've picked up an even bigger following. I think he's saved our cowboy way."

Watching the broody cowboy, Charlotte saw the love in his eyes. A tender caring for his son. "He's saved you too."

"I think you're right. He has saved all of us. He truly is a blessing."

They rode close enough that Charlotte could reach over and give a gentle squeeze to Parker's forearm. "Give yourself credit too, Parker. I've watched your channel for a long time. The guy in the background is normally the one who is pulling the hardest for everyone else. Yes, Chase plays a part too, but he couldn't have done it without you."

"I suppose you're right. I should give myself a little credit."

"Yes, you should," Charlotte said, kicking Rosie to catch up with Garth and leaving Parker to think alone. "Could I borrow your rope for a few minutes, Garth?" Charlotte asked.

Garth puckered out his lips, and he glanced down at his beloved rope. He really didn't want to share, but his dad had taught him better. "Sure. But make sure you give it back. Okay?"

"I promise."

Unwrapping his rope, Garth gave it one last squeeze and handed it to the lady who talked funny. Charlotte gathered the rope and readied it over her head. She swung in over and over her head and then brought it to the side of her horse and back up. When she attempted to swing it on the other side, the rope collapsed and crumpled into a long line, dragging behind her horse.

"Wow. Who taught you that?" Garth asked.

"I did," Parker said, beaming from ear to ear. "You've been practicing."

"I have. Don't worry, Garth, we can practice together. I still have a lot to learn."

"My dad does it real good." Garth turned on his pony to look at Charlotte. "He even has a trick with Blossom."

"He does?"

Parker held his hand out for the rope. Charlotte placed it in his hand and he wound it up, making it look easy. "Once we get up on flat ground, I'll show you Blossom's trick. We haven't shown it on the videos, yet because I still haven't perfected it."

The three horses trudged their dripping wet legs up a rocky wash bed and Parker trotted Blossom a few feet ahead of Rusty. He started by twirling his rope above his head, then around several times to both sides. He then nudged Blossom into a slow jog trot and made his winding loop bigger. He brought it to the side of his mare and bumped his leg for her to move through it. Gently, she hopped her front legs through and Parker guided the rope around with a twist of his torso to her back legs and kept it swinging. He brought it to a smaller loop, stopping the motion and coiled it back up.

"Bravo," Charlotte cheered, clapping at the brilliant show the cowboy and horse had performed. "That was incredible. Why haven't you shown that in your videos?"

"Chase and I have been working to do it together. It doesn't always work out. And Grey is a lot bigger horse than blossom, so Chase has been having a harder time getting him through."

"I could do it, dad!" Garth's little eyes practically begged.

"Why didn't I think of that sooner? When we get back to the ranch, we will start practicing right away."

Garth bounced up and down in his saddle. Parker handed him back his rope, and he tied it to his saddle with the strap. The three of them headed back through the desert to the ranch.

***

When they arrived back at the ranch, Jason was waiting. "Hey guys. I wish you would have told me; I would have love to video your ride. Please don't tell me if anything exciting happened. I might be disappointed."

"No. It was just a normal ride. My dad did his Blossom trick for Charlotte."

Jason brought both hands up to the air space in front of him. "What's up with that, bro? You did it without me?"

Pulling his saddle from Blossom's back, Parker said, "Hey, it was just practice." He shrugged it off as if it were no big deal.

Charlotte followed Parker's every move. She was determined to be a quick study. She pulled the large hunk of a saddle off Rosie and almost plummeted to the ground with it. "Oh, my!" Sighing, she stood back up, grateful she didn't drop it. "I didn't expect it to be so heavy."

Parker was halfway to the tack room when Jason rushed over to the princess. Her back arched as her small arms struggled to hold the thirty pounds of leather. "Let me help you. Sheesh. Parker should have known better."

"No. Thank you, Jason, but I've got to learn this whole ranch thing. I can do this." Charlotte bounced the saddle slightly to readjust her grip.

Holding onto the saddle with white knuckles and tensed stomach muscles, Charlotte followed where Parker had gone. The room smelled of dirt and sweaty horses. The walls here lined with over thirty big, hunky western saddles. They all sat on racks that were hung on the walls in lines to fit as many as possible, from ceiling to floor. "Where do you want this one?" she asked, her back straining to hold it upright.

"Here." Parker was impressed she had carried it that far and hurried over to relieve her from the heavy weight. "I had planned to come back and get that for you." Charlotte allowed him to take it and put it on the rack. Her muscles in her arms and back screamed in relief.

"It was no bother," she lied. Hoping he wouldn't see through the pain in her facial expression, she smiled and winked. Unexpectedly, Parker scooped her with both arms and held her in front of him. She wrapped an arm around his neck, bringing their eyes into a deep stare. Parker leaned in and took her lips with his, softly kissing her over and over. She could feel his heart racing. Tingles of warmth sparking and exploding inside of her made her forget they were in a dirty tack room open to whomever. At any moment, someone could walk in.

Walk in, they did. Charlie was expecting to do a short inventory of the saddles. Replacing any latigos, or stirrup fenders or cinches that might need to be upgraded, when he found his son holding a beautiful woman, practically eating her face off. He cleared his throat. Not that he wasn't glad his son had finally moved on, but he just didn't know what else to do.

The two love birds stopped abruptly. Parker's face gleamed two shades of dark red. He gently released Charlotte's legs, guiding them to the ground. The arm that had wrapped around his back slid down to his waist and stayed there for support. Her head still swirled inside a kissing coma.

"Dad," Parker rubbed at his chin, then quickly shifted, placing an arm around Charlotte too. "I—We didn't hear you come in." He swallowed hard, forcing his head forward. A large lump has surfaced, and he felt as if he were caught in the haystacks, when this type of thing was a big no-no in his teenage years.

"Son, you're a grown man. You're allowed to have an intimate relationship with a woman. Hell, I encourage it. I just wanted you both to know I was here." Charlie held his hand out. "Hello, I'm sorry my rude son hasn't introduced us. I'm Charlie, the dad and the grandpa."

Parker shifted, and his spur clanged. He adjusted his hat, cursing himself for forgetting such an important detail. "Sorry, sir. This is Charlotte, the princess from our European trip."

"Well, I'll be. I knew I had seen her pretty face before." Charlie seemed to stand a little taller. He removed his hat and bent at the waist. "Your majesty, it is a pleasure."

"There is no need for that," Charlotte said. "I'm just the younger sister. Not the queen or anything of that respect."

"You are the closest thing to a queen that has ever set foot on this property and I hope everyone has treated you as such." Charlie lifted an eyebrow at his son. "If not, please come straight to me."

"Thanks for your concern, Dad, but everyone's been great."

"I didn't ask you, Parker, how do you know how she feels?"

Parker looked over at Charlotte. His face softened, and his eyebrows lifted. Had he missed something? Charlotte placed a hand on his cheek. "Everyone has been great. Thank you, Charlie."

"Dad, would you mind helping Garth with dinner and bed? I would like to take Charlotte to dinner."

"Yeah, no problem. You two go have fun. I just need to finish this and I'll go find the little cowpoke."

With a gentle pat and a squeeze to his father's shoulder, Parker led Charlotte back out to put the horses away. He looked for Garth but didn't see him. "Kyle, have you seen the little man?"

"Yeah, he went out on a ride with Chase," Kyle answered.

"Great. Can you tell them both to eat with Charlie and that I took Charlotte out?"

"Yeah, no problem. Have fun."

"So, if you're taking me on an actual date, I would love to shower and change."

"Why would you ever want to do that? You don't want to smell like a sweaty, dirty cowgirl?"

Charlotte pushed on his chest. It felt like a hard wall under her hand. "No, it's not that. I just don't want to smell you."

Parker brought his shirt up to his nose. "I don't smell anything."

"That's because you're used to it," Kyle added as he walked by the two of them. "You should shower, man."

"Thanks Kyle, you're not helping," Parker yelled out after him as he walked off toward the ranch house.

They walked over to the car that David was waiting in. "Can he have you back here in an hour?" Parker asked, nodding to David.

Worried she might have to ride in the disgusting hay truck again. Charlotte struggled to find words to not offend Parker. She knew neither of them wanted to have David chaperone, but she didn't even want to sit in that truck again. "I'm not sure we will stay clean in your truck."

Confused a little, Parker paused. "Aww, you mean the hay truck?" he chuckled. "Don't worry. I'll drive my personal truck. It's a little cleaner." Charlotte sighed in relief. He opened the door to the black car, and she got in. "See you in an hour," Parker said, directing his voice toward David. Who only nodded.

He watched the car drive away. Parker's heart warmed. He wanted to jump up and down, kick his heels to the side and yell 'yee-haw'. It had been so long since he had felt like this. He just hoped he wasn't making a mistake. If this all went right, it would be him, Charlotte, and Garth ranching until the sun went down. His heart soared at the thought.

With those warm feelings, he turned and walked toward the house to shower and put on his cleanest clothes.

Chapter 16 Dinner at Flo's

Rummaging through his closet, Parker found little worthy of a date with a princess. He only owned one pair of jeans that had stayed dark blue. The rest of them were a worn shade of sky blue, had holes, or were dirty. He slid those on and sat on his bench with leather conditioner and a rag to clean off his boots.

After a good wipe down, he examined them. He nodded, a little surprised they cleaned up so well. Satisfied, he put them on. Without a shirt, he walked down the hallway to Chase's room. Chase went out more often and had a larger selection of nice shirts. Borrow and ask forgiveness later, Chase wouldn't mind.

He shuffled through several Hawaiian shirts and a few polos until he came across a black button down with white accent threads. He pulled it down from the hanger and slipped into it. After buttoning it, he examined himself in the mirror. He dragged his finger through his hair and gave a soft whistle. He grabbed his hat on the way out and left the house to find Charlotte.

The black car was outside the ranch house, waiting at an idle. Parker walked up to the back door and opened it. He held his hand out to Charlotte. She took it. Her small hand in his felt more right than anything he had felt in a long time. Soft and comforting.

She had curled her hair in waves. They draped down to the middle of her back, accenting her blue eyes and pink lips. She wore a white summer dress with sunflowers. It clung to her perfect curves and his body shuttered at the thought. Charlotte smiled. "You look good."

"So do you," he said. Fighting the urges to claim her as his own and forget dinner.

"Are you sure, madam, that you don't want me to escort you? I'm not sure your sister…"

"I'm sure, David," Charlotte said, interrupting him before he could finish.

"I'll bring her home. Thank you, David." Parker tipped his hat.

"I'm not sure that is appropriate," David said, right before Parker shut the door.

Still holding her hand, Parker left the black car with David inside and led Charlotte to his pickup. He opened the passenger door and helped her in. As he walked around, Charlotte watched him. A smile spread across his face as he looked at her while crossing in front of the truck hood. Her chest pounded, and she bit her bottom lip. He was the most beautiful man she had ever seen.

When he got into the truck next to her, a leathery musk and shaving cream wafted over her. "Is this truck better than that old hay truck?"

"Much," Charlotte fiddled with a loose hair on her face. "Do you have a place in mind?"

"Of course." Parker drove Charlotte into town. The tension between them was evident by the silence that continued until Parker pulled into a parking spot in front of a diner.

Opening her door, he led her into the quaint building. It was old. Charlotte had only seen diners like these in the movies. Every red and white striped booth had a 5cent coin radio and a straw dispenser with a lifting metal lid. Cakes and cookies were on display behind the hostess desk. The only server was an older lady who wore an outfit that would have only been seen in the sixties. "Just pick any booth you want, my boy," the older lady called out.

Parker picked the same booth he always did.

"On a date, Parker?" the lady asked as she walked up with a pad and pencil. "Oh! Is this the princess from your videos?"

"Hi Flo," Parker greeted. "Yes, the princess from our trip. Charlotte, this is Flo."

"I watched every episode three times, so I could see the two of you kiss, but Jason was never lucky enough to catch it. But I could tell the two of you had something special. Ol' Flo knows." She tapped the pencil to her temple.

Parker hid under his hat. He hoped Flo didn't say too much. On those occasions, he slipped away from the ranch and had breakfast at the diner; Flo always seemed to squeeze out his feelings. He felt safe telling her things. Her advice was normally good. After all, she had been the one to convince him to go to Europe.

"What can I get you kids?" Flo asked, pencil ready. She studied the young couple.

"I wanted the steak," Parker added. "You know what I like."

"I do. What about you, young lady?"

"I guess I'll just have the burger with chips. I mean fries?"

"French fries? They are a crinkle cut," Flo said, looking up from her pad. Waiting.

Charlotte looked at Parker for help. She did not know what a crinkle cut was. "Yes, Flo, the fries are what she wants," Parker assisted. "And a round of waters, please."

"You got it," Flo said, turning on her heels and headed for the kitchen.

"She seems nice," Charlotte said.

"Yeah. I've known her since I was a kid. She owns this place and has run it since I can remember. The food is pretty good too. All home cooking."

"It's nice here. I can see why you love it so much."

"Could you see yourself staying?"

Charlotte placed her hand over Parkers, across the table. "I would love to stay. If I did, would it be ok to bring my horse?"

"Of course. He would have to get used to being out on pasture. We don't have fancy barns like you do."

"I think he will manage. He's a horse. Who knows, he might be happy out there, being a normal horse." Charlotte winked.

Shortly after their talk, Flo brought them dinner. Parker watched the beautiful woman in front of him and his mind soared through the clouds. He imagined her in a beautiful wedding gown, its white laced train flowing behind her. Garth holding a small pillow with the two rings on it. Was this really happening? She had agreed to stay. Did this mean she was ready to tie the knot too? He made a mental note to go into town in the next few days to find a ring.

They finished dinner, Parker drove her back to her hotel and walked her to the door. "Thank you for dinner, Parker. I think crinkle fries are a new favorite of mine."

Nodding his head with a small chuckle, Parker agreed. "Pretty much anything Flo makes is good. Next time, if we aren't so full, we should try the carrot cake. It takes four hours to make from scratch. It might be the best thing my taste buds have ever experienced."

Charlotte leaned in and kissed the cowboy on the lips. Inhaling his leathery musk, she said, "Mm." He cupped both sides of her face with his hands, pulling her in for a few more kisses. "Good night, Parker. I'll see you tomorrow."

He tipped his hat and waited for the door to close before he threw it up in the air. It spun a few times. He caught it and placed it back on his head. He could run three marathons, ride a bucking bull, and still not satisfy the feeling he felt. His body exploded inside with new love. He felt he could jump into the sky. The clouds didn't feel high enough; maybe he'd make it to the moon.

Parker went to bed that night happy. He knew exciting things were coming his way. Garth would finally have the family he deserved. Not that Chase and Charlie weren't great, they were. He just wanted Garth to have a mom-like figure in his life, too. One to help heal the wounds his biological mom had caused him. Charlotte could be that for him, making their little family circle complete.

***

The next morning brought a few surprises. Parker was up early, grabbed a quick glass of orange juice for breakfast and headed toward Garth's room. His little man had already left. A tingle of pride made Parker smile.

Heading toward the ranch house, he noticed Chase on Grey. His rope was out, and he was practicing their giant loop walk through. "I still think Grey is too big. Maybe just borrow a smaller one from the pasture?"

"What? Are you kidding me? I couldn't do that to Grey. It would hurt his feelings. Besides, the fans would miss him."

"Alright, whatever you think. Hey have you seen Garth?" Parker asked as he looked in the tie area and didn't see Rusty or his son.

"Yeah, him and Charlotte took the first customers out already. Jason went with them."

"Charlotte?"

Chase groaned as he twirled his rope, the large loop strained his arm as he attempted to nudge Grey into it. One of his front legs caught the edge, and it failed. "My man, she is in it to impress. She was up and saddled before I could say good morning."

Parker's eyebrow flew up to his hairline. "No one helped her?" He took off his hat and scratched his head. "And she took out customers with Jason? So, this will all be on film?"

"Yup." Chase was now coiling his rope back up, ready for another round. "Hey, I've got an idea. Can you help lead Grey through with a treat or something? There's a bag of peppermints in my truck."

"You bought peppermints for the horses?"

"No, just for Grey. For when he's a good boy. It gives him nice breath."

Chuckling, Parker headed toward Chase's truck. A small Honda drove down the driveway toward the parking lot at an insane speed. The tires slipping as the driver made the slight turns of the road. "Idiot," Parker shook his head back and forth. "I'm going to have to have a talk with whoever that is."

Parker opened the door, grabbed the bag of candy, and popped one into his mouth. Just as he shut the truck door, the Honda pulled into a screeching stop, bringing a mountain of dust quickly after. He waved his hand back and forth in front of his face, scowling. "What in the name of..."

Out of the car popped Briel. "Why hello there, cowboy."

Parker's heart skipped a beat or two. The blood in his veins went cold. What was she doing here? If he had never seen her again, it wouldn't be soon enough. He didn't want Garth to see her. It would shatter the boy. Confuse him. They had seen so much improvement. He was happy. And that same shy boy he met the night she dropped him off was now the most vocal guy at the ranch.

"Are you just going to stand there and stare?" Briel waved her manicured nails over her lady lumps. "Like what you see, pretty boy?"

Parker rolled his neck and ran his tongue over his teeth, making a sucking sound when he finished. His heart beat a million miles a minute. He didn't want her here. "Why are you here Briel?"

"To make things right, of course," she squeaked and bounced her body. His eyes could not miss the jiggling melons that she had paid money to attach to her chest. Not that he didn't like them, but for her small stature, they didn't look right. It made her appear unbalanced.

"Make what right exactly?" Parker narrowed his eyes.

"Why us silly? Our little family. Now that you've gotten to know our son. We can be what you always wanted." Briel dropped her purse. The ruffled skirt she had on was so short it was more of an inside the bedroom costume. She winked and turned, trying to tease him, but he looked away. What had happened to her? What had she been through that had changed her so much? He pitied her. She was not the mother he wanted for his son.

What had happened to her singing gig? Had she been so willing to run off, and leave Garth for something that was short live? What did she want?

He reached for her shoulders when she rose from picking up her purse. Trying to avoid the boobie-traps she had practically hung out of the shirt that looked three sizes too small. "Briel, listen. We don't need you. I—Well, you've changed. I've changed and I have someone I'm dating. So, there can't be an 'us'. You can't expect me to wait around while you parade around like a…" Parker motioned his hands up and down in front of her, making sure to not touch her.

"Like what exactly, Parker?" Briel hung her head to the side, dipping her shoulder to get a little closer to him. "What exactly do I look like?"

"Well, I don't want to offend," he said, hanging his head and shuffling a boot against the gravel.

"Like a whore?" Briel shoved his shoulders, catching him off guard as he stepped back a step. "You made me this way! This is your fault. I had to do what I had to, to survive."

"I was willing to take you and the baby six years ago, but you left. You left, not me," Parker said, pointing to his chest. "You are just as much at fault. And I don't want you to see Garth. It will only hurt him."

Briel threw up her hands and circled, her high heels grinding into the dirt. "You can't keep me from my son!" Briel stood on her tippy toes to look over Parker's shoulders. He didn't dare take his eyes off her, for fear she may dart toward the ranch house. "Oh, so there is your little hussy. And with my son, no less. No wonder you don't want me around. You've already replaced me."

Garth led the customers into the tie area, his little mouth running like a motor. Charlotte followed right behind him, smiling. She was elegant and charismatic. Parker could see that their guests had a lovely time. Charlotte was the perfect fit and now Briel was here to ruin it all.

Trying to push Parker out of the way, he stopped Briel. "Listen, Briel, please don't make a fuss in front of our guests. You'll only embarrass yourself."

Again, she shoved him. He stumbled to the side and watched her aggressively stomp her heels. He rubbed at his forehead. "What in hell's tarnation have I got myself into?" he mumbled under his breath. He turned and followed her a short distance behind, praying she wouldn't make a mess of things.

Luckily, Chase and Jason took the customers over to the side for a photo shoot. Charlotte had dismounted and was helping Garth tie Rusty. "Hi baby," Briel said. She opened her arms.

"Mama!" The boy ran to his mother. His little arms wrapped around her bare legs and the ruffles of her skirt smashed into his face. "Why did it take you so long?"

"I just have to get a few things sorted out. I'm here now." Briel smirked, looking straight into Charlotte's eyes. "And your daddy and I are getting back together, so we can have the family we've always wanted."

A dryness took over Charlotte's mouth. Her head dizzy with spots, she placed her hands on Rusty to steady herself. With a few breaths to regain her composure, she held out her hand. "Hi, I'm Charlotte. You've got a wonderful boy."

Briel didn't take her hand. She only looked down at it. Staring like Charlotte had offered her a disease. She ran her fingers through Garth's hair, keeping her hand busy instead. Charlotte recanted and rubbed her hand on her jeans. "I was just visiting the ranch. I didn't know you lived here too."

"Well," Briel rolled her eyes, "it's relatively new."

By now, Parker had reached them. "What are you talking about? Briel, we haven't seen you in months. And you're not staying."

"No! Daddy, please don't make her go away again," Garth said between tears. "Please, Daddy." He held her tighter, hoping she wouldn't leave this time.

"Garth." Parker froze. He looked into Charlotte's eyes. He could see the hurt, the betrayal. The cowboy was stuck. There was only one option; losing Charlotte or making his son unhappy. There was no having both at this moment. He would have to hurt one of them and pray to the all mighty above he could fix it later. "Garth, mommy can stay for tonight."

That was all it took. Charlotte's jaw tensed. Pausing for only a second, she shook her head and left toward the parking lot. Leaving her horse still saddled and tied to the post.

"Charlotte, wait!" Parker called after her. "Thanks, Briel." If looks could kill the look he gave his ex, would have sent her flying a hundred feet backward. A fall she wouldn't have come back from. "I wish you would have stayed away."

Before he ran after the princess, he glanced down at his son. His little lip quivered. How could his dad do that to him? He knew how much his mother meant to him. She had come back to fix everything, and he didn't understand why his dad couldn't just make their family whole. It was something he had always wanted.

When Parker caught up to Charlotte, he grabbed her arm to stop her and bring her to look at him. Her eyes were damp and swollen. "Charlotte, please. I didn't know she was coming. I haven't thought twice about getting back with her."

"Parker," she said, staring at the ground, doing her best to hold back the tears that threatened to surface. "It was stupid of me to come here. To think I could get in the middle of you and your son. I'm sorry."

"No. It's not like that. I want you to be our middle. I want you to stay with me and Garth. Help with the ranch. Bring your horse here."

"I can't break up a family, Parker." She looked into his brown eyes. Tears trickled down his dirty cheeks. "I'm sorry, it just can't work out. Thank you for teaching me how to be a cowgirl." She placed a hand on his cheek, rubbing a few of the tears, he leaned into her.

"Please," he whispered. Parker removed his hat and dropped to one knee. "Please, stay. Marry me? Please." He begged with his hands in a praying position.

"No, Parker. I can't." With that, Charlotte turned from him, opened the car door, and stepped in. "Drive David." She watched the handsome cowboy through the dark window tint, knowing he couldn't see her inside the car. His shoulders drooped, and his robust face went weak and wet from tears. Her heart hurt for so many reasons. She was stupid for coming and thinking she could have a chance. She turned to look at Parker one last time. He had fallen to his knees, his hat lay on the ground, and he held his face as he cried sobbing tears.

That was when her heart shattered into a million pieces and the proud princess, who'd been taught to never show weakness, also cried.

CHAPTER 17 COWBOY TUFF

The following day, Parker buried himself in his work. Briel had stayed on a cot in Garth's room. Garth gladly showed his mom everything he had learned in the past few months. Chase assigned Kyle to take the two of them on a trail ride to help give Parker some space.

Chase found Parker in the hay barn stacking hay. "Hey, man." Parker ignored him. "You know, the hay was fine how it was."

"I just wanted to move it to this side. Before the monsoon. It will stay dryer that way."

Biting down on his lip, Chase stuck his hands in his pocket. "I'm sorry about Charlotte. I'm here if you need me."

"Thanks Chase, I'm fine." Parker kept moving hay.

The shot of rejection brought heat to his face. Chase's first thought was to throw angry words back at his friend. Something calmed him. He knew Parker was hurting inside and the last thing he needed right now was his bestie giving him a lecture.

Instead, he walked to where his brother was and grabbed both his shoulders and forced his sweaty body into an embrace. Parker fought Chase only for a moment and then his body melted. He buried his face in Chase's shoulder and cried. Chase rubbed his friend's back for comfort.

"I can't do this again, Chase." Tears and clothing muffled Parker's voice. "I can't choose Charlotte over Garth. And I can't break his little heart again and send his mother away."

"You're one of the strongest guys I know. I look up to you. It's because of you I can act like a confident idiot on our videos. Garth will survive without Briel. Unfortunately, she is his mother, so we can't completely shut her out." Parker sniffed, lifted his head and wiped his nose. Chase looked his friend in the face. "I've made an appointment with the lawyer. We can talk to him about custody and put a restraining order on her from coming onto the ranch because she was threatening our business."

"That all sounds great." Parker sniffed again. "But we can't afford that."

"Yeah, Park we can. After our Europe trip and Garth. We can. Those two things have saved the ranch. We write it off as a business expense. We need Garth and he needs us even more. I've seen that boy grow so much in the last few months."

Parker rubbed his eyes. "I've grown into such a wuss. I've cried way too much to call myself a cowboy."

"Only tough guys can cry and get away with it." Chase pressed his lips together. "I think you're going to have to repent for letting your hat sit on the ground intentionally, though."

Parker lightly punched Chase on the chest and chuckled. "Yeah, I can burn it later."

"Come on. Let's get you cleaned up. We have an appointment in an hour at Flo's."

Together, the two cowboy friends walked off toward the ranch house.

***

A few hours later, Parker and Chase returned from a lunch and meeting with their lawyer. It went better than Parker had expected and it was the most hopeful he had felt in the last twenty-four hours.

As they walked back to the ranch house, Parker noticed Briel sitting under a large cottonwood tree watching Garth ride his pony. Kyle was pulling a roping dummy, and the boy was doing his best to rope the horns. She stood up as they neared. "Where have you been?"

"Wouldn't you like to know?" Chase spouted off.

"Actually, yeah."

At least her backside was covered with a pair of jeans, Parker thought. Her shirt was only a tube that ran horizontally across her torso. Had it been several years back, Parker wouldn't have been able to keep his hands off a woman dressed that way. She knew what she was doing. She knew that no man could resist looking. Briel was a beautiful woman, small, fit, shapely, especially with her newest additions. She also knew how to get what she wanted from a man.

Little did she know Parker had changed. Recovering from the trauma she had caused him had made him see life differently. It helped him grow into a stronger man. Life wasn't a joke. He had grown up, and he didn't have time for petty games from a woman he could never trust.

"Briel, I've met with a lawyer. I had him drawn out paper for custody of Garth, with holidays and visiting rights. You can make any adjustments by calling him."

"Parker, you can't be serious?" She moved in closer to touch him. He backed away.

"I won't play your games anymore. With me or Garth."

Chase nodded. Proud of his friend for standing up to her.

"This isn't a game. This is our lives. Our son's life."

"I also filed a restraining order against you for entering the property here on the ranch. You're allowed to pick up Garth on his days, but you're not allowed to exit the car."

"Are you kidding me? Are you threatened by me? You pompous pig!" Briel spat at Parker's boots. "I'm taking the boy with me."

Parker held out a large envelope. "And by order of the court, you're not allowed to take Garth unless he agrees."

"This is ridiculous!" Briel stomped her foot. "You can't do this to me."

"Actually, he can," Chase added. "It's all here, in this stack of papers." Chase grabbed the papers and forced Briel to take the packet.

"Parker, please don't do that. I can give you a far better life than that wench. She isn't your son's mother." Briel tried again to reach for him. She threw a small tantrum when he once again backed away. "I've changed. I know leaving you was a mistake. The biggest one I have ever made."

"Yup. And you get to live with that mistake for the rest of your life. Have a nice day Briel. Say goodbye to Garth. I doubt he'll want to go with you. Let my lawyer know which holidays you prefer." Parker tipped his hat and left. Chase followed.

"You'll be sorry, Parker Hawkins!" she yelled after them.

"I doubt it." He looked over at his friend. Chase patted his back. "Man, that felt good."

"I'm proud of you, man."

"Thanks for always being there for me, Chase." Parker walked toward his son in the arena with Kyle. "Garth, ride on over here."

Kyle drove the quad with the green plastic cow attached, and Rusty followed. "Hey buddy, your mom can't stay here. She hasn't been nice to me and we are afraid she may not be great with the customers. I know this will be a hard choice for you, but I need you to be strong. You need to decide if you want to stay here with me, grandpa and Chase or go back with your mom."

The little boy's eyebrows furled together. "I don't understand why she has to always cause problems." He looked up at his mom, who was now walking over.

"What are you saying to him, Parker? Are you brainwashing him?" Briel yelled. She stopped across from Parker and Chase and placed a fist over each hip.

"No, I think he just needs to have a say in this. He gets to decide. I'm not keeping him here if he doesn't want to stay. If he prefers to go with you, then so be it." Parker turned to his son. "You are always welcome home, buddy. You will always be *my* son."

Garth reached down and patted his pony on the neck. He looked at his mother, tears in his eyes, then looked at Parker and Chase, who stood relatively close to one another.

"I can't believe you'd let a six-year-old kid make a tough choice like that. He couldn't even wipe his butt by himself two years ago." Briel stroked her son's knee. "Remember baby, mommy took care of you."

Thinking long and hard, Garth remembered moments where his mother had left him with strange people, sometimes overnight when she had promised she would come home. He loved his mother, but he also knew she didn't always keep her word. It had happened too many times. She had let him down. He wanted to forget how scared he was. He wanted her to stay with him so he could show her what a tough cowboy he had become. It was Parker who showed him how to be happy again. Parker was a good dad, even though he'd only met him a few months ago.

"I want to stay with dad," Garth said, looking straight into Briel's face.

"Why baby? I've always done what I could to take care of you."

"Because, Mama, you don't always come back. You leave me just like you left Daddy. And it hurts too much. Daddy doesn't leave me."

Parker and Chase both watched Briel. She was speechless. The kid spoke the truth, even if it was brutally honest. Parker was proud that his son was wise enough to see how his mother really was. She had hurt him in the same way she'd hurt Parker, and he recognized it.

A storm cloud thundered inside of Briel. She turned on her heels, and like lightning, she slapped Parker across the face. His head spun to the side with the force. "I hate you!" Galumphing off to her car, she got in, slammed the door. She rolled down the window. "You can have your stupid cowboy of a son!" The tires spun, sending tiny rocks in all directions as she skidded across the parking lot and onto the road off the ranch.

Garth sighed. "I don't miss her bad tempers."

"Garth buddy," Parker said. "Come here." He held out his arms to his son as he dismounted. "I'm so proud of you." Parker took the small boy into his arms and squeezed him tight. "I love you, son. You know I will never leave you. Don't let her mean words hurt you."

"I know Daddy. You have a good heart, like me. I knew I didn't get it from her."

With a smug smile to hold in the tears from flooding, Parker looked over at Chase. Chase brought his arms out to wrap them around his boys. "Good riddance to her."

"Yeah," Garth added. "We don't need her. She told me she was here to take the ranch. Because she wanted me to have it and give her the money."

"She said that to you?" Parker asked. The boy nodded. "You know, I'll teach you everything, and then one day, the ranch will be yours. Without her trying to steal it from me."

Garth shrugged.

"You will be the roughest and toughest cowboy. Together, we take care of all the animals." Parker ruffled the boy's hair. "And when you're old enough, you can teach your son how to be a rancher, too."

The little cowboy laughed and pushed his dad away. "Stop Dad, you're silly." Garth stepped on the tire of the quad and climbed back onto his spotted pony. "Come on, Kyle, I need to rope this green cow some more."

"You got it, boss," Kyle teased. "That's one hell of a kid," he said to Parker.

"He's a better man than I'll ever be."

The two cowboys walked into the ranch house and grabbed a drink from the small cooler and plopped onto the dirty couch that sat in the middle of the room. "Boy, it's been a rough few days," Parker said. He set his hat down and hung his head back over the edge of the couch.

Chase sat down next to him and a puff of dirt clouded next to his legs. "This couch needs to be retired."

"That's why it's in here. No one cares."

"It doesn't impress customers," Chase said, then took a sip of his soda.

Laughing, Parker brought his head up to look at Chase. "It's intended for sweaty, smelling cowboys to take a few minutes off their feet. Have you brought customers on this couch?"

"Maybe." Chase Shrugged. "They normally get grossed out once I lay them down on it."

"Gross, man. Too much information."

"You're just jealous."

"Maybe. I think I'm done with the opposite sex for a while. I need to focus on Garth."

"Speaking of the female counter-part. I think we should book a flight for you and Garth to bring Charlotte back." Chase took another sip. "She was good for him and you."

Parker sat up straight. He fiddled with the tab on the top of the can. "Do you think she would listen?" He groaned as he thought about the day before. "I tried man. I even proposed to her."

"Yeah, but it wasn't the right moment. And you didn't have a ring. You can't get the girl without the ring, my man. That is so backward."

"I'm an idiot. Aren't I?"

"Maybe a little, sometimes." Chase braced for a punch Parker almost laid on him.

"You really think it's worth a try?"

"I do. After I saw how much she meant to you yesterday. Yeah, I do." Chase placed his empty can on the glass table in front of the couch. The aluminum clanged. "Plus, it will be great video footage."

"You want to record that moment?"

"Duh. All of our fans are rooting for the two of you. You should have heard the three I took out the other day. They were practically taking bets when the wedding was and where."

Parker leaned over, placing his elbows on his knees, and rubbed vigorously at his temples. "I can't believe I'm even considering this."

"A man will do stupid things when he's in love," Chase patted Parker's back with a few hollow thuds. He rose from the dirt filled couch and left Parker to think about what they had discussed.

CHAPTER 18 BACK TO THE TEAHOUSE

Parker and Garth sat on the airplane watching movies and taking naps for over nine hours, when the pilot came over the intercom and said, "This is your captain speaking. We will land in about twenty minutes. The current weather is clear with a temperature of twenty-two degrees Celsius. Thank you for choosing to fly with us. We hope the rest of your trip involves safe travels."

The fasten seat belt sign dinged and Parker helped Garth buckle in. The little boy had been asleep and his head still hung in a groggy state. "Almost there, buddy."

Garth yawned. "She told me she lived very far away. And that's why she didn't bring her horse."

"Yeah, it's hard for horses to travel that far. Sometimes they can get shipping fever and die."

"Oh my. That is scary."

"It can be."

"Do you really think she will want to be my mom?"

Parker had told Garth that Charlotte or any other woman could never replace Briel. She would always be his mother. He explained to his son that Briel couldn't live with them on the ranch. She would always be like an eagle, flying from place to place, never able to stay with them for a long period. He and Garth would miss her, and wish her best on her ventures, whatever they may be.

"She would be crazy not to. If she doesn't, she has her reasons and we will have to accept that," Parker told him.

Once the fasten seatbelt sign dinged and cleared them for boarding off the plane. Parker stood and pulled the two small carry-on bags from the top compartment and sat them on the chair. They didn't plan to stay long. He patted the small black velvet box in his front pants pocket for safekeeping and helped Garth out of his seat.

They pulled out the handles and rolled their bags through the plane and out of the airport. Parker rented a car and drove to a small hotel in the village near the castle. The same one they had ridden in carriages through and stopped in the teahouse for a quick lunch.

It was past noon, and father and son were starving. Parker only knew of one place, so he helped Garth clean up and they headed to the teahouse.

As they walked up the familiar path, Garth couldn't help but touch the flowers. "I've never seen flowers like these. It's so pink, and that one is purple! Look Dad, a blue one, my favorite color."

"I thought maybe fairies lived here," Parker teased, sticking a finger in Garth's side, making him giggle.

"Stop," he begged. "I don't think Charlotte should leave here. It's too pretty."

They entered the house-like restaurant. The hostess smiled and asked, "Two today?"

"Yes, please."

She brought them to a small table that sat two, right by the window. Garth was looking out the window instantly, admiring the side gardens. She poured them a mug of tea and placed biscuits in a basket in the middle of the table. "Dad, I know why Ms. Charlotte is so pretty."

"You do?" Parker took a sip of his tea. "Why is that?"

"It's because it's so pretty here. How can you come from somewhere like this place and not be pretty?"

Parker nodded. "I think you're right, buddy. Wait until you see the castle."

They finished a late lunch of soup and a sandwich and left the fairy garden teahouse. "Do you want to go see the palace today or wait until tomorrow?"

"I think we should go today, Dad. Cowboys don't wait around. Let me see the ring again." Garth reached for his dad's pocket. "Yup, I think she's going to like it. It's really sparkly, like the flowers here."

Father and son left the teahouse and headed out of town toward the castle. Slowly, the countryside opened; towering trees, rolling hills, and miles of green grass filled their view. Garth had never seen so much green in his entire life. There was no doubt in his little mind that anything that came from this place was special.

It was a good twenty-minute drive out of town. With the long travel and a full belly, Garth fell asleep. Parker's heart was throbbing. His lungs felt heavy, and he tried to take long breaths to control himself.

He reached an arm over and gently shook Garth to wake him. "Hey Buddy. We are here." Garth shuffled a little. Only waking enough to toss his head in the opposite direction. "We made it, Garth." Parker tickled the little boy's nose this time.

Garth reached up and swiped his hand away, and then vigorously rubbed the itch away. "I think the car made me sleepy."

Parker chuckled. "Come on Bud, get up and get moving. You'll wake up soon enough." He still felt sick to his stomach. The chance that she might reject him again was too much. He held onto the steering wheel, gripping it so tight his knuckle bones in his fingers bulged out under the white skin. He could just turn around and go home. Take Garth for a brief vacation and never take the risk.

"Are you coming Dad?"

"Yeah—Yes. Let's go find Charlotte." Parker shook it off. Got out of the car and headed toward the castle.

Garth grabbed onto his dad's hand. "You were right. This house is the biggest house I've seen. Does she live in there?"

"She does. Her sister is the queen."

"The queen?" Garth looked up. If he hadn't had been holding his dad's hand, he might have fallen over. "Wow." When they finally reached the biggest wooden door Garth had ever seen, his eyes widened. "Does a giant live with them?"

"Hah! No, a big castle needs enormous doors, or it would look funny." One of Garth's eyebrows raised with this thought. "Did you want to knock? I'll lift you to reach the metal ring right there." Parker pointed at the knocker.

"Hmm, ok."

Parker lifted the boy and Garth reached out and tapped the ring. "Harder dude. You've got to get all the way through that solid door." The second time Garth made sure the metal ring in his hand made a loud hallow sound. "That's my boy!" He set him down.

"It's taking a long time," Garth said, with both hands at his hips.

The door opened. It moaned on its hinges, flashing Parker back to the first time he had entered that palace. He hoped this time they wouldn't get kicked out. The same older gentleman greeted them. "Welcome to the palace. Can I help... Oh, I almost didn't recognize you without your hat, Parker. How may I assist you and your little friend here?"

"We are here to see Princess Charlotte."

"She's a princess?" Garth questioned. Parker gave his son a quick wink.

"Aww yes. She is out on a ride this afternoon. It is possible you may find her in the covered riding arena."

"Thank you. We'll head that way." Parker tugged on Garth's hand. His heart raced once more at the thought of seeing her again.

"Dad, slow down. You're walking too fast."

"Sorry. I'm a little nervous."

"Why? Because she's a princess and you're a cowboy?"

Parker ruffled his boy's hair. "That's one reason."

As they neared the barn, that seemed to Garth like a three-mile walk. Parker stopped. "Did we go the wrong way?" Garth asked, looking up at his dad.

"No. Buddy. Daddy's just not ready."

"It's ok, Dad. You've got me now. We are braver together."

Parker kneeled and gave his son a squeeze. "Thanks, Bud. You've given me all the strength I need."

They walked hand in hand into the barn. He inhaled the aroma of wet arena dirt with a sprinkle of woodchip musk. There, in the middle of the perfectly manicured arena, was a beautiful horse and rider. The two boys stopped, watching the rider and horse dance. Together in complete unison to the beat of the music that lightly played in the background.

Inhaling and taking deep breaths, Parker walked toward the white fence that lined the arena. "It's ok dad, I got your back." Parker smiled at the boy. Sweat dribbled down his back and down the sides of his freshly shaved face; burning the skin a little.

They watched Charlotte ride a few times around on her big brown gelding until she halted in the middle. It wasn't until then she looked up to see the two of them standing there. Watching her. Her eyes widened. The gelding shifted under her quivering body. She nudged the horse forward. "What are the two of you doing here?"

"We came to see you," Garth told her matter-of-factly.

"You did, did you?" Charlotte steadied the gelding, who didn't want to stand and talk non-sense. "Are you just in the neighborhood to say hi or?"

"Why is your saddle so funny?" Garth squinted his nose at the small nothing of a saddle she sat on.

Parker laughed and ran his fingers through his hair. He watched the sapphire in her eyes, admiring him. He pulled at his chin and looked at Garth to save him from this moment. Garth only smiled at his dad.

"Your horse is like two Rustys. I can see why you didn't want to get him on a plane to Arizona. Plus, I think he would hate all the *cactuses* since he's used to all this green stuff."

"You might be right," Charlotte agreed. "What does your dad think?"

"I think anyone can adjust to change." He shrugged, making himself feel more awkward. "We just came to get you. I mean, we missed you and thought maybe you missed us and maybe you'd want to come back?"

"I already told you, Parker," Charlotte's eyes quickly whipped to Garth and back to him, "I can't do that."

"Why don't you want to be my mom?" Garth pressed his lips together and stomped his foot.

Charlotte's eyes flicked back to Parker. Where had Briel gone? She left Arizona so she wouldn't interfere with their family. "Did I miss something here?"

He knew there would not be a better time. Garth had already made the reason they had come obvious. He pulled the small black velvet box out of his pocket, dropped to one knee, and flipped it open. Inside was a shining diamond ring. The Princess's face turned a shade of white. Her gelding pawed the ground as he felt her heartbeat increase.

"Charlotte. Garth and I want you to be part of our little family. We know we aren't perfect and there might be hard times, but," Parker winked at Garth, "we think you can—You make us better." Parker bit down on his bottom lip. "Will you marry me and make me the happiest cowboy ever?" Garth tapped his dad's shoulder. "Oh sorry, will you make us the happiest cowboys ever?"

Tears welled in her eyes. She chewed softly on her bottom lip, wanting more than anything to say yes. To feel Parker hold her again. To kiss her again. Smell him. Her heart sank. Would this be something Mary would agree to? "Can I put my horse away first?"

With a flick of his finger, the velvet box clamped close, and Parker stood. His mind grew fuzzy. Spots filled his vision. He watched her ride the horse away toward the side of the arena that led to the barn. He reached over for the white fence to brace himself as his heart dropped out of his chest and splatted on the ground. That wasn't the reaction he had hoped for.

Parker huffed out a small whimper. He still held the fence with both hands, his head hung between his shoulders. The small box dropped to the soft dirt with a poof. "Dad? Are you ok," Garth asked. He placed a small hand at his dad's side.

"Yeah." Parker stood upright. "I just didn't think she would say no." He sighed out again. His knees shook, and he swallowed the bile that wanted to surface. He couldn't deal with the rejection. And he couldn't have a breakdown in front of Garth. "Come on buddy, let's go."

"But dad," Garth pointed to the box on the ground.

"Leave it."

Garth grabbed his dad's hand, and they left the barn and headed toward the car. Leaving Charlotte behind from their lives forever. Parker didn't waste any time. He drove straight to the hotel, grabbed their bags, and headed right back to the car for the airport. He couldn't stay in this humid, green place any longer. It hurt too much. Reminded him of her. He needed to forget love.

Focus on Garth and the ranch and shove his feelings aside. Women made him weak. He felt like an idiot for listening to Chase. Chase had been wrong.

CHAPTER 19 MOVING ON

The ranch was a great distraction. It was hard work. Work that never ended. It had been a week since Parker and Garth flew back to Europe to make the biggest mistake of his life. Twice, he asked Charlotte to marry him. He would never make the mistake of asking her again. He explained to Garth on the plane ride home the reason she couldn't say yes. Charlotte had official duties to tend to with her country. When deep down inside, he knew it was him. He had pushed her away. The lack of skills with the female gender had caused this. She had tried to make it work. She had come all the way to America and his stupid, stubborn pride got in the way.

Garth was a little sad, but was over it quickly when he was back in the saddle, helping customers on Rusty, and helping Jason make videos. With Chase's charm rubbing off on the boy, he was going to be a superstar by the time he was sixteen. Parker only hoped he learned Uncle Chase's skills with women and not his own.

With the ranch finally on the financial mend. Charlie planned to throw a party in honor of Chase and

Parker's success. They had over two million subscribers and brought in enough money now to help keep the ranch a float. They invited anyone and everyone.

Charlie hired a DJ, and Flo's to cater the BBQ. She closed out the restaurant for the evening just for the event. Parker helped Garth shower after a long day of riding and work. "Why do I have to get clean now? I'm just going to get dirty out there," Garth complained.

"Because we have to get our nice clothes on and smell good for all of our fans." Parker put hair gel in the boy's hair. "And you don't want to smell bad for your fans, right?"

"I didn't smell bad."

"You can't always smell yourself. I smelled you, and you didn't smell good." He reached down and tickled Garth in his ribs. The boy wiggled like a worm on a hook. "You smelled like you rolled around with Rusty in a stall filled with sweaty manure."

"Ew!" Garth moved away from his dad and slicked down his hair. "I don't need that crap. I'm wearing my hat."

"Ok. I was just trying to help." Parker waved for him to come back. "Now let me finish with those buttons."

"I can do it, dad. You smell too. Go shower."

Parker laughed. "You're right I do. Why don't you go help Grandpa while I clean up?"

The boy finished with his buttons and stuffed his shirt in under his big belt buckle and ran off. Parker shook his head and smiled. He was glad to have Garth in his life. He just hoped he could be as good of a dad as Garth was a son.

After cleaning up, Parker joined his dad and Garth in the kitchen. Chase walked in just as he sat down at the high-top-bar. His arms were full of one large, brown cardboard box. "You guys ready for this?"

"What is it?" Garth asked, his eyes as big as two moons.

"I ordered us all new matching boots!"

Garth leaped down from his chair and ran over to Chase. "I want mine," he said. He jumped up and down, hardly able to keep his excitement in.

Chase shuffled around in the box, making sure Garth couldn't get a peek. He pulled out a small pair of western boots. "I had them carve the toe here," he waved around the front of the boot, "barbed-wire and I designed the long piece that goes up your leg as the American flag. Even better, look at the bottom." Chase held the boot up to show the three of them. A horse, two cowboys, a little guy and a cow through a clear, rubbery-like substance showed visible like a professional cartoon sketch.

The boy pulled his pant legs up one at a time, pulled his current boot off and snatched the new boots from his uncle. "These are so cool. Thanks Uncle Chase." He paraded around the living room. Skipping and hopping like a proud stallion, his new boots practically shining.

"Here Parker," he held out a set, "these are yours. I've got a pair for Jason and me, too. I thought it'd be fun for us to take a picture later."

"Thanks. Can never have enough boots. Besides, mine are getting a little worn out."

"These are for fancy occasions. Not ranching boots."

Parker eyed the boots in his hand. "Aren't they just boots?"

"Very expensive boots." Chase pulled out his pair, turning them around. "I'm thinking we could market these."

"You think people would buy boots with us on them?"

"Uh, yeah. Because it's us. Put 'em on. Let's get out there to the party."

Everyone helped bring the rest of the events last minute necessities from the house, outside. People had already gathered, and they flooded the ranch with chatter, music, and tables. They had a small stage set up in front of the tie area for the DJ and a designated dance floor with no tables around him. Jason helped line up the parking. He waved his arm around as each new driver entered the ranch, lining them up through the empty land they had that led to the ranch so they could fit as many guests as possible.

Flo's had prepared smoked pulled pork, chicken thighs, cowboy beans, cornbread, and a creamy mac and cheese. She kept her carrot cake hidden for later in a refrigerated unit they had towed behind one of their trucks.

So many people in his place of comfort made Parker's stomach feel like a roller coaster. Garth was eating up all the attention he could get. He watched his son travel from one person to the next. Whatever he was talking about seemed to keep the people entertained with smiles and laughs.

Parker grabbed a plate of food and had planned to eat out in the far pasture with Blossom when a guest grabbed his arm. "Parker," she swooned. "Oh, my gosh. I can't believe it." She shook her head. "Sorry, I'm just nervous. You're like so famous. And now that you are free from any relationships. Would you like want to grab a coffee? I'm here in town for the next week. I even have a trail ride booked in two days." She placed her fists in front of her face and squealed. "I'm so excited. Do you think you will take me or Chase? I totally want…" Parker lifted an eyebrow and swallowed deeply. "I'm rambling, aren't I?"

His eyes only glanced down at her hand that still held onto his arm. He grinned, trying his best to not make the situation any more awkward. "I—Uh. I will have to check the schedule."

She slowly removed her hand, leaving red and white finger marks where she had gripped him so tightly in her excitement. "Oh, sorry about that." She bit on her lip. "Ok, well, I really hope it's you. There's room at our table if you need to sit." She motioned back to where her friend sat. They waved. Parker nodded his head to acknowledge them. They wiggled and cackled between each other.

"I've got to go check on the horses," he thumbed over his shoulder, "ya know, just to make sure they are dealing ok with the crowds and the noise."

"Oh right," she said and scurried off to her friends.

Now that his food had gotten cold, he sighed. He continued his walk to the pasture, this time with a brisk walk to avoid any more distractions. He hopped the fence one handed, balancing his cold plate of food perfectly, and sat down next to his normal tree in the open field.

Sending out one whistle to Blossom to let her know he was there before he sat down to eat, Blossom lifted her head once and put it back down to graze again.

Even cold, Flo's food was music to Parker's taste buds, smoky goodness in every bite. He had decided that mac and cheese had some secret magic dust in it, because it was out of this world with cheesy cream.

When he had finished, the knots in his stomach returned. He would have to venture back to the mass of people soon. He rolled his fork and napkin up on his plate and stuffed it in his back pocket. He grabbed the halter that sat on the fence and placed it on Blossom. She wasn't happy about leaving her grass and he had to tug on her lead rope. "C'mon girl, it's show time."

He led her to the back of the ranch house, where they had stashed their saddles for the evening. Chase was there with Rosie. "I thought you had ditched me?" Chase said. "I almost put Miss Rosie back to retrieve Grey for a cattle demo with Garth."

"Nope, just went to get Blossom." Parker tied her and brushed her down. Puffs of dirt and grass flowed off her coat. "You've done a great job showing Garth the ropes with the customers."

"He's a natural showman. I saddled Rusty first, and he took off to show his roping talents."

"He did?"

"Yup." Chase chuckled. "He couldn't let us have all the fun."

Once the two cowboys had saddled their mares, they headed toward the music and laughter. As they neared, the DJ announced, "Thanks for the roping demonstration, Garth. Everyone, let's give this talented kid a hand, before we let our next two stars onto the stage." With one last hooray, Garth stood up on his saddle seat, and took a bow and tipped his hat before he plopped back on to his pony.

"Everyone, we give you Parker and Chase." Claps, cheers, whistles, and yee-haws overpowered every sense. Garth rode Rusty over to join them. "Good luck guys," he said.

"Thanks buddy." Parker smiled at his son and nudged Blossom front and center.

Chase opened their act. "Just so everyone is clear, we've been practicing this for a few months. And mostly because I wanted to be riding Grey, but he was just too big for what we were going to show you. So instead, Miss Rosie gets to have a little spotlight." He cupped his hand to the side of his mouth. "Don't tell Grey, he might get jealous." Laughter circumvented among the crowd. He nodded to the DJ to start the country music.

The two cowboys reined their horses next to one another and, circling around the small area in a canter, they brought out their ropes. The twirling rope started small, but soon became a giant loop. They split off down the middle, so the horses loped in opposite directions. Chase nodded across the arena to Parker, and the giant loop angled down in front of both horses. Almost in perfect sync, the two mares cantered through the circling ropes.

Parker's heart secretly leaped inside of him. The trick couldn't have gone any better. They just had to do it one more time. They continued to lope around and when they again met opposite sides of the arena, Chase nodded and the horses hopped through yet another perfect swinging loop. Slowing the two horses they met in the middle brought their ropes to a coil on their saddles and took a bow at the waist.

More claps and cheers. Parker cooed to Blossom as she danced in place, spooked a little by the noise. Garth joined them and the three cowboys lifted their hats, yet to another round of screams and whistles.

As they quieted, they brought their hats back to their heads. Parker nodded to Chase. "We can't thank all of you enough. To those of you who are watching this at home who couldn't attend today, and to those of you who are here." He swallowed back a tear. "To my brother Parker and his amazing son, to Charlie and Jason. We couldn't have done any of this without you." Chase reached over to Parker. "We can officially say you've all helped us save the cowboy way."

Parker grabbed his hat and lifted it again. "Now go eat that cake that Flo spent hours making for us, get on this stage and dance your hearts away! And keep watching our videos." The three cowboys turned and left the center stage. The DJ started up the music, and the people merged onto the dance floor.

"Do you think Grey will ever forgive me?"

"Yeah. Give him some extra grain tonight. He'll forget all about it."

They unsaddled the three horses and put them out to pasture. Garth took off like a lightning bolt toward the cake, promising to race Chase and eat his slice too. Chase gave a smug look to Parker. "I guess I better hurry before that boy eats all the cake."

"Save me a slice, will ya?" Parker watched Chase run off, catching up with Garth. He grabbed his waist and swung him in a circle. Parker didn't want to go back into the crowd of people. He knew he should, but he just couldn't find it in himself. So, instead, he walked toward the hay barn to hide and enjoy a little time to think, away from the loudness of the party.

He climbed to the top of a half stack, placed his hat carefully next to him, and leaned back. He stuck a long piece of hay in this mouth and curled his arms behind his head to rest on his hands. Relieved the evening was almost over, he closed his eyes. The music, laughter, and chatter in the distance gave him a peace of mind. All pieces in his life had finally resolved. Briel had disappeared again. She would probably have a dramatic entrance at some point, but at least they had prepared Garth.

Parker had dozed off. The stress of the party, the performance, and the long day had exhausted him. His dreams were cruel. The sound of her voice was so real. "Chase told me I might find you here." He smiled a little, feeling his body waking he kept his eyes closed, hoping she would keep talking. "I had hoped I'd find you with your shirt off again."

This time, she felt too real. He pried one heavy eye open, two beautiful blue eyes hovered above him. His body reacted so quickly, he sat up, causing her to topple over off the first stack of hay he laid on and onto the lower few bales. "Parker!" she screamed, and she rolled.

Leaving his hat, he quickly peered over the edge where he thought he saw Charlotte fall over the edge. "Charlotte?" Hay covered her dark brown hair and flowered summer dress. Her smooth skin showed up to her knees. A small prickle of excitement warmed him.

She did her best to dust off the hay. Still flat on her back, she started laughing. "I had planned this all out.

It never goes smoothly with you, does it, Parker Hawkins?"

Parker covered his mouth with a fist and shook his head. "No, ma'am, it certainly does not."

"Are you going to help a lady up?" she asked, glaring up at him.

"I'm still trying to decide if you're real or if I'm dreaming."

"Would it be a good dream if you were?"

Parker's face melted into a dreamy state. "A magnificent dream."

"In that case, you better get down here, because climbing in a dress isn't easy."

Parker didn't hesitate. Leaving his hat behind, he bounded off the taller stack of hay, landing more gracefully than the princess did. He bent over and offered her a hand. "My lady?"

Charlotte took his hand in hers. It felt so right as he laced his calloused fingers over hers. A quirky grin filled her lips, and she pulled the cowboy down. He briskly toppled over her, catching himself with his hands on either side of her shoulders. "I thought I had a better balance," he said, his cheeks blushing.

"I put you where I wanted you," she said. She ran a finger over the line of his hairline, tracing it. Her touch softened him. He leaned in and kissed the soft lips he missed. Lips he knew he should never kiss again, for fear of breaking his heart once again, but his body ached for her. Pieces of his heart warmed as they mended together with every movement their mouths met.

"Do. You. Still. Think. You're. Dreaming?" Charlotte asked between his sweet kisses.

"Definitely." He leaned to his side as his arms tired and pulled her body closer to his. "Rolling around in the hay with you can be nothing but a dream."

"Would it make it better if I told you yes?"

Parker stopped his kisses that had now traveled down her neck. His body was now on fire, and she was lucky to have said something to stop him, because if this was a dream, he was going to take her; his way.

He leaned up on his elbow. He pulled a few pieces of hay out of her hair. "Are you sure?" He grabbed another and chucked it to the side. "Has Mary approved?"

Charlotte sat up. Her smile gleamed from ear to ear. Biting over her bottom lip, tears welled in her eyes. "She has, and we've even sent over my horse. He's in quarantine until tomorrow. So, I really hope you still want me?" She released a small huffy laugh. "Because it was very expensive to bring him here."

"Charlotte," Parker's voice cracked. He took her face in both of his hands. "There would be nothing more I could ask for. Garth will be so excited."

Parker kissed her a few times around her lips. Each time she tried to catch one, but he was too quick. Her body trembled under his touch. "Did you miss me and my kisses?"

"Yes," she moaned out. "Please."

"Please what?" he teased.

"Please don't…"

Gently, he rubbed her face with the back of his hand. He knew he had to stop now or he wouldn't be able to if he continued. "You never told me your horse's name."

Charlotte sat up straight. "I didn't?" Parker shook his head. "His name is Cappuccino. But I call him Cap."

Standing up and offering a hand to her, he chuckled. "That's a silly name."

The princess shrugged.

Parker hopped back up to retrieve his hat and grabbed her hand. "C'mon, let's go announce our news."

"In front of everyone out there?" She pointed toward the party.

"Yeah. Why not?"

"Are you ok with that much attention?"

"Darling, I want the world to know that you're mine." He kissed her on the cheek. The blush on her face carried on through her neck and down her spine, making her shiver.

They walked back toward the party. Parker had never felt so invigorated in this life. His step popped, and his chest puffed out, proud to hold a princess he would soon call his wife. He could take on any crowd with ease, because his insides now bubbled confidence.

No one noticed when they walked up to the DJ. The cowboy whispered something to him and he left his perch. Parker led Charlotte into the stand, tapped the microphone, and the music stopped. "Excuse me, I would like to make an announcement." Every eye on the property focused on them. For a moment, his heart froze, but Charlotte squeezed his hand, reassuring him he wasn't alone anymore. He glanced over at her. "I've asked Charlotte to marry me, and she has accepted."

The audience roared. Parker backed out of the DJ stand and he returned to play a slow song for them. Parker led Charlotte to the dance floor. He took her in his arms and swung back and forth. She laid her head on his shoulder. Shortly after, people joined them.

"When you came a few weeks back. I had wanted to say yes. I just needed time to talk to Mary. You didn't have to run." She looked up and met his eyes. "I thought... I had hoped you would have stayed. I wanted Mary to meet Garth. I went to sleep crying that night. Broken, that I might have missed my chance."

Parker kissed her forehead. "It was Mary that came to my room that night. She held me in her arms, like my mother used to. She told me we couldn't help who we fell in love with and she would not be the one to keep me from it. I made her a promise in exchange that we would visit from time to time."

"I can do that. It's a small price to pay for you, I suppose."

She batted his chest. "You suppose?"

"Is the queen going to pay our travel expenses?" he teased.

"Yes. She agreed she would pay."

A little tap on Charlotte's elbow made her look down. "Excuse me, ma'am? Could I have this dance?" Garth gave his dad a smug glance. "Sorry Dad."

"She's all yours, little man."

"Hello Garth," Charlotte said to the boy. "Are you ok with me being your stepmom?"

"Yeah, I tried to tell my dad he shouldn't give up so easy. But he just gets so nervous. His leg bounced up and down on the entire plane trip to you. He even tried to go back home a few times. I knew you wanted to be my mom, though. My dad is a just a big chicken. So, it's good you're going to marry him. He needs all the help he can get."

Charlotte chuckled. "I'm honored to be a mother of such a brilliant young man." She winked at him and smirked at Parker, who was watching on the sidelines. "We can help him together. Family is a team effort."

Chase walked up to the man he called brother and patted him on the back. "Well done, my man." He brought him in for a side hug. "She's going to keep us all in line."

"I hope so, because we sure need it," Parker said. "I haven't felt this happy in a long time, Chase. I don't even know where to begin. My heart is so full, I don't even know what to say."

"Park, you never know what to say. Don't mess it up this time, ok?"

Parker shook his head back and forth. "I sure hope not."

"You'll be fine. If she lasted this long with your sorry broody arse, she'll stick around." Chase fist bumped Parker in the cheek and walked off to flirt with the pretty cowgirl he had now gone on a few dates with.

Happiness swarmed him as he watched his boy twirl Charlotte around. The flowery summer dress waved around her knees as she bounced around the dirt with his—their son. His heart wanted to burst, sunshine beaming from every pore even though it was after dark.

"Son," Charlie said, walking up next to Parker. "I couldn't be prouder of you."

"Thanks Dad."

"I think you better hold tight to that one and never let go."

"I agree, Sir."

When the song ended. Charlotte and Garth joined Parker in eating a piece of carrot cake. It was already

Garth's third piece, but Parker let it slide this time. Charlotte placed her hand over Parker's. "It feels right, doesn't it?"

"It does."

Garth leaned over the table and placed his hand over Charlotte's. "And I'm just happy to have a woman around these parts." He shook his little head back and forth, brazing Parker in the face with the tip of his hat. "Because there are too many cowboys around this ranch."

Chapter 20 Epilogue- One Year Later

Garth sat between Parker and Charlotte on an airplane bound toward Europe. Charlotte looked down at the ring on her finger and smiled. She shifted in her seat, the growth in her waist band made sitting for long periods of time hard. Garth looked up at his stepmother and she smiled. He reached out and patted her round belly gently. "Do you think we can name her Reba?"

Parker chuckled.

"Is there a reason you chose that name?" Charlotte questioned.

"Well, I was named after a country star, so my baby sister should be named after one, too."

"That's a noble reason." Charlotte ruffled his hair. "After the baby shower at the palace, we can mention it to Queen Mary. It's tradition that the queen help name the first baby in our family."

Garth sighed. "Daddy said Queen Mary didn't like cowboys. I don't see why we have to go all the way to see her."

A quick glance from Charlotte to Parker told him he would be in the doghouse later. He looked away into the aisleway carpet, scratching at his chin. "Let's take you to the bathroom, Garth," he suggested, hoping his wife would forget the subject.

His sister-in-law Mary wasn't his favorite person. He knew Charlotte had promised they would visit; he had just hoped it wouldn't be so soon. Mary insisted upon giving her sister a baby shower in the palace. Parker had tried to convince Charlotte to go after the baby was born, but she wanted to go before. And there was no way he was going to let her travel alone, so here he was stuck on a plane with his son and his miserable, cranky, very pregnant wife.

Once Garth had finished in the bathroom, Parker gently kneeled and reminded his son that his mother was edgy. "Remember how we talked about Aunt Mary and that Mommy loved her?" Garth nodded. "So sometimes we have to not say things that Daddy says about her. Sometimes Daddy needs to remember to keep those things to himself."

"It's ok Dad. I understand. You're not perfect." Garth nodded his little head and pressed his lips together. "But I'll still keep our man to man talk between us."

"Garth." Parker's face softened. "Sometimes I think you're too wise for your age. I think you should have been the dad, not me."

Garth held up his hands to his side. "But then, who would have taught you?"

Chuckling, Parker agreed. He watched the boy walk ahead of him and shuffle into their seats. As he approached, he looked at his beautiful wife and saw the love in her eyes. Her smile softened him and he realized how important it was that they had this time together as a family. Even if Mary most likely would boss him around the entire time. Charlotte was worth every moment. Garth had a mother now that loved him more than life. She was an example of everything he wasn't. She had stuck with him even when he was a stupid cowboy, on more than one account.

"Garth, come here a moment. Switch seats with your mom." Parker offered a hand to help Charlotte stand. She struggled with her basketball sized tummy protruding outward. Garth peered out the window and Parker helped his wife sit back down. He laced his fingers through hers and kissed her gently on the cheek. "I love you. And I'm sorry I was negative about Mary."

"Thank you," she said. "And it's ok, I know how my sister is. We will get through this next week together. At least this time, she can't tell me to stay away from my cowboy."

"Cowboys," Garth corrected her. Charlotte had given him a reason to trust her. She hugged him all the time, she went on horseback rides when she wasn't pregnant, and she promised she would never leave him in the car. "Because I'm your little cowboy, and Daddy is your big cowboy."

She grabbed Garth's hand with her free one. "Yes. You're right. My two cowboys." She bent over with a grunt and kissed the boy on the head. She rubbed her belly and Garth placed his head over her hand.

"I can hear her Mommy," Garth said, with a giant grin.

"She can't wait to meet her big brother. You can teach her all the cowboy things."

"Yes, but I don't know if I will share Rusty. She needs to get her own pony."

Charlotte smiled at Parker.

"We will see," Parker said. "She's going to have to earn herself a pony." He poked at his son's ribs and he giggled. "Just like you did."

Parker finally realized the only way he could have ever truly saved his father's ranch was with the help of these two people. Not only did they save the cowboy way and the ranch, but they saved him, too.

The End

Stephanie B. Whitfield

Authors Note

Stephanie enjoys writing, reading, and riding her horses in her spare time. She is a multi- genre writer. Thanks to her supporting husband and friends who encouraged her to share, writing has allowed her to give a bit of her magic to the world one story at a time.

Her works include: a Young Adult Urban Fantasy- Hidden in Roll trilogy, a witchy short story- The Repercussions of Magic, and a kindle Vella story called- Buckles and Bulls. All published and available on Amazon. Stay tuned for the up-and-coming High Fantasy: The Sword of Moira.

Enjoyed this read? Check out my other books on Amazon and/or on my website and be the first to know what's coming next by joining my newsletter, where you can be the first to be informed on new releases, special offers, giveaways and free reads. Join below by visiting my website below.

www.Stephaniebwhitfield.com

If you enjoyed this book, please leave a positive review on Amazon, Goodreads and/or Bookbub. Authors rely on reviews for success. It doesn't have to be long; short, sweet and simple is great too.

If you would like to follow me on social media, you can do so with the links below.

FB- https://www.facebook.com/authorstephaniebwhit

IG- @authorstephaniebwhit

ACKNOWLEDGMENTS

THANK YOU--

To my daughters Navie and Lila, who have listened, supported, and read my pages out loud with me, giving me tips and good laughs. My son Wyatt, who rolls his eyes at mom's books.

To my supportive friends Bonnie Kokona, Carrie Bryce, and my mother-in-law Bonnie Whitfield for being my incredible editors. My sister-in-law, Joanie Whitfield, for her constant support. These amazing people gave me endless hours of reading and constant uplifting thoughts.

My cover designer Thia—She is awesome, patient, and a true pleasure to work with.

To my cousin Katrena King for always being willing to read. And last to my ARC readers: Kali Stewart Shaw, Susan Stradiotto, Elena Carter, Heather Weir, and Rebecca Lange, I couldn't do it without you.

Last but not least, my husband Jared, for putting up with my silly stories, my horses, and book collecting.

www.ingramcontent.com/pod-product-compliance
Lightning Source LLC
Chambersburg PA
CBHW011852300726
48970CB00009B/2764